The Echo of the Mountain

Kyle Born

Cover Art by Manu

Based on real People

in a real Place

PART 1

~

I

Isaac sat up on his bed. He was ready to leave his old home, but uncertainty in the unknown was equally potent. Either way, he was slow to get out of bed and even slower to begin loading the wagon. He eventually filled it with wooden boxes of clothes and rations. Then, he piled a rope, a hat, and his father's old army revolver on top.

It was the summer of 1877: seven years since Isaac's father was killed on the trail to Fort Benton. By the time his body had been found, wolves had torn him apart while flies swarmed. No one really knew exactly how he died, but many knew the name John Cohen. During the Civil War, he was a major under George McClellan and one of his most trusted friends. Had he not decided to begin a family in Nevada City after the war, he would've received an accelerated promotion to Colonel. Nevertheless, he moved to Nevada City where he based his expeditions into British North America. These explorations prompted more fame from the detailed maps he returned with.

Despite John's death, his wife Mary Cohen decided to keep Isaac in Nevada City for the foreseeable future. The commission money John had left behind was enough for a decent life, which was all Mary hoped for.

But by 1877, Nevada City was almost abandoned, and Isaac was tasked with riding their old nag to Virginia City for food and other goods. Though the journey was tiring, Isaac enjoyed his trips to Virginia City. There, he could see friends and watch the townsfolk amble around the street.

Mary Cohen was not as content with their arrangement, and when offered a cabin in Bannack by an old family friend, she took it. Mary was not a hasty woman, but she was lonely. Ever since her husband passed, time had become very apparent to her. Her bright demeanor was ill-suited for a life of isolation. Isaac too, though he wouldn't complain, was eager for a new setting. He was only ten years old when his father died, and as such, their Nevada City residence became a constant reminder of his absence.

Isaac finished with the last of their things and called his mother to the wagon. "I doubt the nag'll make it to the Twin Bridges," he laughed to Mary. Their wagon was small, but the uneven road was a challenge for even the most expensive horses.

"Well we ought to getcha a new one in Bannack. I hear they have a breeder in town," she said.

"If we make it that far," Isaac replied.

Isaac admired his mother's optimism, but even she couldn't push away the perils of the road. Their journey would take two days according to Orsdel, the Cohen's friend in Bannack. William Van Orsdel was a funny, reserved man who served as a traveling Methodist preacher. John Cohen had known Orsdel for a long time, and they had reunited in Fort Benton when John was returning from an expedition and Orsdel was preaching. Raised a Methodist, John had sought Orsdel's council throughout his life to keep him at peace. In John's letters home, he referred to Orsdel as "Brother Van", a nickname that would stick with Isaac. John even gave Orsdel a map of where the Cohen family lived in Nevada City, should he ever need a place to stay. And on a windy winter night in 1873, a freezing Orsdel showed up outside the Cohen home hoping to relive the good times he'd shared with John. After finding out about John's passing, the evening was filled with nostalgia. Isaac, Mary, and Orsdel went around telling stories around the fire about John until everyone was too tired to keep a fluid conversation. That was not the only night Orsdel stayed with the Cohen's over the next four years, and in 1876, Mary received a letter of invitation to move to Bannack.

Orsdel had purchased a small parcel of land on which to build a church and cabins for himself and perhaps the Cohen's. Many years ago, Mary had read about Bannack becoming the Beaverhead County seat and the capital of the Montana Territory. Although both titles were given to different mining towns within the year, it displayed the prominence of Bannack, which was just what Mary wanted.

With a sluggish grunt, the nag set off toward the distant mountains. The path to Bannack took them northwest up to the Twin Bridges, then southwest down to Bannack. The entire day they had a mountain range firmly to their left. Had Isaac not needed a wagon, he continued to believe he and Mary could make it up the ridge and down to Bannack in a day.

"It's pretty dark," Mary said, looking at the stars in the night sky.

"Well," Isaac responded, holding up his dim lantern, "Let's keep a move on until we find somewhere a little less–"

"Rough?"

"Yeah," Isaac laughed. "That'd be a good idea." A mile later Isaac pulled the nag under a tree and began setting up their tent while Mary checked one of John's old maps for landmarks. She noticed the tall pine they were sheltered by was accounted for by a thick dash. Tracing her finger up the path and down from the Twin Bridges, she noticed a scribbled box.

"Isaac, come over and look at this."

"Maybe it's a homestead?" Isaac replied quizzically.

"Maybe," she muttered, folding the map back up. "I'm going to try to get some rest. You should too."

"Night," Isaac said as Mary climbed into the small tent. He then found a soft tuft of grass and fell asleep gazing into the night sky.

||

Isaac woke to the buzzing of flies over his head. He slashed his hands in the air to disperse the pests and got dressed. The nag was as lethargic as ever, and they were all hungry for something to eat. Mary pulled out some dried pork and handed it to Isaac while he packed up their things. Soon after, they set the nag up front and started toward the Twin Bridges.

Unlike the previous day, it was not at all sunny. The path was covered in a dense heap of fog. Isaac felt little water drops form on his hands as they rode through it. They reached the end of the mountain range in no time and crossed the Twin Bridges before noon. At this point, they began to shift their direction from northwest to southwest.

Isaac reached behind him and brandished his father's old Colt from the wagon. With time, its beaming metallic finish had corroded. He examined the inscribed *JC* on the grip. Although he never got to meet his grown son, John Cohen made sure to teach young Isaac everything he knew about life. One of these lessons was the proper etiquette and handling of a revolver and repeater; two things John had mastered in the army. Isaac practiced dry firing the old revolver until John deemed him ready for ammunition. At this stage, Isaac could crack old bottles at a distance of a few dozen feet. He advanced to moving birds, and soon, he became somewhat of a gunslinger himself. But hitting targets by flipping and twirling a gun was never his style, he let his learned accuracy speak for itself.

As the Cohen's continued down the road, Isaac couldn't help but think about his father's death. How had a man so talented with a firearm been killed by bullet wounds? The doctor in Fort Benton had examined his father's corpse and assumed a lost duel, or something of the like. But this resolution never satisfied Isaac, it simply didn't make sense.

Out of nowhere, there was a loud bang in the air. The wagon came to a halt. Isaac looked at his body, wondering if he'd been shot. He quickly examined a panicking Mary, but neither of them were injured. But then he heard the horrendous screech of the nag, squirming in pain. Soon, the wagon was off the trail and the nag loose. It galloped a couple of feet before falling into the tall grass, dead. Isaac shoved Mary under the wagon and looked around for the gunman.

A second later they were shot at once more, this time the bullet grazed the wagon Isaac was hiding behind. Mary began silently crying.

"It's going to be okay, Ma," Isaac whispered.

Another bang revealed the gunman's location. There was a subtle cabin off to the left of the path, before the slope of the mountain range began. A masked figure was aimed at them from the roof of the dilapidated structure with two hitched horses standing idly below him. The fog was just thin enough to give the man a clear view of the wagon but not the trees behind them. After the next bang, Isaac set off running to the forest behind them. Mary remained still, her eyes transfixed on Isaac's movements.

From inside the forest, the gunman was barely visible. Isaac crept around the curb of the forest's edge to make his way to the cabin. Ninety feet. Eighty feet. Seventy feet. Isaac's eyes darted to the cabin window. He noticed a flickering oil lamp sitting next to the glass. He pulled up his arm to aim.

"Breathe," he mouthed. He pulled the hammer back and shot the wooden wall. The bullet missed the oil by a foot. Five more shots. Isaac took another deep breath. Mary had figured out Isaac's plan and began reaching for the repeater stashed in the wagon. Isaac stayed focused on the lamp.

"Breathe," he begged, his hands now sweating. He cocked the gun and released another shot into the glass frame of the window. The gunman shifted his gaze to the edge of the forest and took blind shots into the fog. The bullets hit the trees around Isaac, but none connected. Another bullet zipped past Isaac, and this time, he returned fire. Stepping out into the open, he sent three bullets up at the roof. Keeping his eye on the roof, he lowered his arm and unleashed a final shot through the lamp, unleashing a plume of fire. The room inside the cabin was soon aflame. Isaac backed up to the treeline as smoke whirled out of the cracked window.

While the gunman was distracted with the brewing fire, Isaac ran up to the building's hitching post and jumped onto one of the horses. He jutted his heels into its ribs and yelled for Mary to grab on, but it was too late. The gunman had descended his post and shot the horse somewhere in the rear, throwing Isaac into the dirt. The animal collapsed in agony right onto Isaac's left leg. As the gunman approached, Isaac struggled to pull out his leg from under the horse. He reached at his back but couldn't feel his Colt anywhere on him.

"Mister, please. I don't know what you want, but let us pass. We can forget this ever happened!" Isaac pleaded from the ground.

"This is the Innocents' territory, my boy! You will pay the price for your trespassing!" the man howled.

"We've got rations! Take what you want, but leave us alone!" Isaac suggested eagerly.

"Well now we're talking!" the man cheered. "Just tell that woman of yours to get out from behind that wagon, and I'll be on my way!"

Before Mary moved, there was a loud infantile cry from inside the cabin. The man turned. "Looks like the new owner isn't too happy about that fire you made, boy!"

Isaac pursed his lips and flipped his head back toward the wagon. Mary slowly stood up with her hands behind her. She took a deep breath, tears still drying on her face.

"Well look at her!" the man snickered at Mary. "Is that your mama, boy? Come over here, honey!"

"Shut your mouth!" Isaac spat.

"You're a fiery young lad," the man said, kneeling down to Isaac. He reached back his hand and slapped Isaac, instantly leaving a red mark on his face. Isaac recoiled and crumbled back to the ground. He could see Mary walking over to them at the edge of his gaze. There was a subtle clanking sound as she approached. "There she is!" the man yelled. "Could you come a little closer, honey? My eyes aren't what they once were."

Mary shivered then took another step forward. The man looked her up and down. He sauntered over to her. Just as the man got close to her, she immediately removed the repeater from her back and pressed the barrel into his abdomen. She fired twice. Isaac finally released his leg and ran over to embrace her. The man convulsed in the dirt as blood poured from his insides, and Mary started weeping.

"The child," Mary whispered. "Get the child."

Isaac swung around and dashed to the burning cabin. The structure was engulfed in flames. He kicked down the door and glanced around for the child. He squinted at the corner of the cabin, where he saw the infant boy wailing. Next to him was the fresh corpse of his mother, her face still pink. Isaac took a deep breath from outside then ran to the boy. He dodged the flames and scooped the crying child into his arms. Outside, he and the boy took turns coughing up smoke while Mary tried to fasten the remaining hitched horse to the fallen wagon.

Soon, the roof was billowing smoke into the sky. Isaac carried the child over to the wagon and set him down. He then helped Mary organize their fumbled belongings. They both climbed up on the wagon in silence. With a quick whip of the rope, the new white horse set off down the path. As night fell upon the family, Mary smiled: "John, let's call him John."

— — —

The rest of the night was uneventful. As the family closed in on Bannack, the flat terrain became ridden with hills and valleys. Over the past several hours, Isaac had witnessed his mother become attached to the orphaned child. Consequently, Little John had stopped his persistent crying and began to gaze at their path ahead. He was a rather small child with big blue eyes and pale blond hair. It seemed he wasn't the talkative type, if he could even talk.

They climbed the steepest hill yet, and after, Bannack was finally in their view. The main street sat a short distance from Grasshopper Creek. All the way through, houses and stores stood beside the street. Towards the end of the main street, a second parallel street jutted out from behind a church. Outside of the main part of town, tents were sprawled across an open valley. Although there were only a few people out, the incredible display of light over the area revealed the hundreds that called Bannack home.

"Any idea where we're headed?" Isaac mumbled.

"In his letter, Orsdel said the cabins were behind the church," Mary responded, eyes still on Little John.

Isaac got off the wagon and led the horse to the church. It was an extraordinary structure: it was taller than any other building and was stained a uniquely dark brown color. They went behind to church to find a little cottage with a smaller home beside it. Isaac noticed a man reading by candlelight within the cottage. He knelt down and crept up to the window. ·

"Brother Van!" Isaac yelled as he reached the window. The man jumped in his chair and ran out to greet Isaac.

"Oh Lord! You scared me, my boy!" Orsdel smiled. He shifted his eyes on Mary and the staring baby. "Why hello, Mrs. Cohen! And who might this young lad be?" Orsdel asked.

"This is Little John," Mary paused. "An orphan from the road."

"Well," Orsdel said, bending down. "It is nice to meet you, Little John. I didn't know I would be expecting three, but your cabin certainly has enough room."

"This is lovely," Mary said, stepping into the home. "I don't know how to thank you for this, Orsdel."

"Don't!" Orsdel laughed. "Think of it as a favor to your husband. He was very hospitable to me on many occasions, so I feel it right to do the same."

Isaac tied his horse to the post near the cabin door and began unloading their belongings from the wagon. It was a cozy little place: there were two beds next to the lit fireplace, a tall table for food preparation, and another table with chairs across from the fireplace. After Isaac brought the last box in, he started to feel at home. He extinguished the two oil lamps on the table and fell asleep to the crackling of the dying fire.

III

Isaac woke up to the sound of a dog barking outside the cabin. He guessed it was the late morning, because Mary and Little John had left. There was a knock on the door. Isaac rushed into his clothes and opened it.

"Uh, are you a 'Mr. Cohen'?" a boy asked at the door.

Isaac laughed, "I suppose so, but you can call me Isaac."

"Well you can call me Kit," he grinned. "Mr. Orsdel asked me to see about stablin yer white horse there."

"Oh, right," Isaac looked over at the mare. "I guess there isn't much space for her inside here," he remarked, gesturing towards the cabin.

Kit had ragged brown hair that matched his worn garb. Despite this messy appearance, Isaac was relieved to meet someone close to his age in this foreign area of the territory.

They both walked out to the mare. Kit patted her back and examined her hooves. He then took her lead and began walking toward the stable at one end of the main street. Isaac followed behind them and observed the bustling town. There were many different kinds of folk that Isaac noticed. Prospectors carried their pans and shovels toward Grasshopper Creek. Wealthy gentlemen wore fitted tophats and luxurious jackets. Merchants unloaded boxes of product from their wagons.

"Did ya hear about the Indian attack?" Kit shouted behind him.

"Err—no. What happened?" Isaac asked.

"Well, they say them Indians been goin town to town killin people in the territory," he said nonchalantly.

"That why he's there?" Isaac said, pointing at the armed man on the hill behind the stable.

"Yeah, that'd be Buck Stinson, Deputy to Sheriff Plummer."

"That sheriff get much action here?"

"Sure, the town's full of outlaws," Kit explained. "There's a gang called the Innocents that've been stealin from travelers near here."

Isaac twitched. "My mother and I ran into one of them on our way here."

"You don't say!" Kit said, intrigued. "What was it like?"

Isaac sighed. "We were ambushed. The man was on top of a cabin firing down at us."

"Huh. What happened next?" Kit asked excitedly.

"They aint above snakes," Isaac said, walking away from the stable. "We picked up an orphan from inside the cabin."

"Well, you must be one hell of a fighter, defending your family like that."

Isaac forced a laugh and thanked Kit for taking the mare. He then continued on his way toward the crowd, but before he made much progress, he saw his mother holding Little John next to a shop.

"Ah, Isaac, there you are!" she exclaimed, ushering him into the building. "Come meet Dr. Leavitt, he was just helping me with Little John."

Dr. Leavitt had been sitting behind the counter of his apothecary when Isaac walked in. He was gray-haired but didn't seem feeble. He wore a long black jacket and had on a pair of glasses. There was a pep in his step as he strolled toward the family.

"Isaac, it is so very nice to meet you," he declared.

"And you," Isaac said with a nod.

Mary began engaging Dr. Leavitt in a quite boring conversation, so Isaac took a moment to look around the shop. The counter was centered at the back of the shop with rows of shelves surrounding the room. The shelves contained all sorts of odd vessels carrying different liquids and pastes.

Just then, a young woman with long sandy hair walked in carrying a pile of books as tall as she was. She wore a lengthy blue dress and muddy brown boots.

"Here's those books you asked for, Doctor," she said.

"Indeed! Thank you, Ms. Darling!" Dr. Leavitt shouted from the other side of the apothecary as she exited. Dr. Leavitt paused for a moment, then continued his conversation with Mary. "That Ms. Darling is really something," he said. "In her breaks from teaching, she helps me with the store."

Dr. Leavitt was still complimenting Ms. Darling when Isaac left the shop to introduce himself. "Hello, miss," he said, panting from his jog to her.

"Yes? Who are you?" she asked, focusing on the crowd as they walked.

"Well," he said, smiling at his feet. "I'm Isa–"

Ms. Darling grabbed him and pulled him into the alley. She swiftly pulled out a knife from her dress and pressed it onto his ribs.

"Listen," she warned. "I don't know which one of those bastards sent you, but you better leave town before you end up *drowning* in the creek."

"I don–" he stuttered, reaching for his absent Colt.

"Oh forget it, let's get this over with," she said, raising the knife to his throat.

"I haven't been sent by anyone! That was my mother in the shop!" he blurted before she could stop him. She maintained eye contact though deep in thought.

"Hmm," she said, covering her knife and pulling back her long hair. "Well, uh, I'm Lucia."

Isaac sank to the ground as she walked away. He had more threats on his life in the past day than he'd had in his whole life. After spending a few minutes deciphering what Lucia had said, he crawled up and walked toward the stables.

To his complete surprise, Kit was busy talking to the very same girl who had almost killed him moments ago. They were smiling at each other. Kit looked down the street and nodded while Lucia kept talking. She seemed concerned, or maybe it was just agitation. When she left, Isaac snuck up to the stall Kit was sweeping.

"Hey, cowpoke," Isaac seethed. "You didn't tell me about the deranged girl in town."

Kit burst out laughing, holding onto the post to stand straight. "Lucia just told me about yer little encounter," he chuckled.

"Yeah?" Isaac challenged. "She's mad. Completely off her mental reservation!"

"Well," he began. "If you had been the murderin type, which I don't think ya are, you'd be the third person this month to try her life."

"And why is that?" Isaac inquired.

"It's not for me to sayl, but if ya see her again, I promise she'll be a little less wild," he laughed.

Isaac appreciated Kit's humorous disposition but was still concerned about the girl. With the sun beginning its slow descent, Isaac made way for his cabin to sort his things.

It didn't take long for him to realize his Colt was gone forever. He scrambled through the boxes with no luck. Perhaps it was still on that trail, decaying in the summer heat. Isaac soured at the thought, and in his cloud of despair, he left the home and made way for the gun shop on the other side of town.

The sun was now low in the sky, and people were gathering in the saloons. He glared at Lucia as she accompanied Mary and Little John across the main street. They seemed to be heading for the *creek*. Isaac hurried up toward the gun shop on the other end of the main street. He glanced over at the empty Sheriff's Office across from the shop and then entered.

"Afternoon," he said to the rough man at the table.

The man looked up with a jut. "Guns or bullets," he grumbled.

"Colt. Single action."

"Don't got none."

"Any?" Isaac pressed.

"Look, boy," the man snarled. "I don't have any, so buy what I got or get outa my shop."

Isaac pointed at a long-barreled revolver on the wall behind the man. "What about that one?" he asked.

"Double action Colt."

"I'll take it." he said with a faint smile.

The man raised his eyebrows in boredom and gathered Isaac's bills. He warned Isaac not to loiter, but Isaac was already running toward the creek. Isaac loaded the shiny gun and placed it in his back waistband.

He hid behind a nearby townhouse and slowly crept toward the creek's edge. He couldn't see Mary or Little John yet, but he could hear Little John shrieking emphatically. After gathering up his courage, he jumped out from behind the wall and promptly drew his new revolver. Only after his gun was aimed at Lucia did he notice her playing with Little John near the water. Luckily, Mary was talking to Orsdel a little distance away and didn't see Isaac's regrettable display of bravery, but Lucia seized the opportunity to make fun of the act.

"Woah there, cowboy," she joked. "You weren't going to shoot me for playing with your little brother were you?"

"He's not–" he began. "Just stay away from us."

Isaac placed his gun back in his waistband and picked Little John up from the water. Lucia might've said something else, but Isaac kept walking away. He dumped Little John in Mary's arms and said goodnight.

The next day started early. Orsdel came over just after sunrise to talk with Isaac. Over the course of the church's construction, many had become interested in their own spirituality and the forgiveness they might feel. This left Orsdel in need of a hand during services.

Isaac wasn't too keen on the idea of being an acolyte. When he was young, their family regularly attended a small church in Nevada City. The pastor's faith was strict. His modeled devotion was quite influential on young Isaac, until 1870.

After his father was killed, Isaac found no solace in the church. He turned away the pastor's efforts to meet with him. Isaac would wonder where God was when John Cohen was gunned down on that trail.

Long ago, when Orsdel first met Isaac on that snowy evening, he did not preface himself as a preacher. He was simply a man: a man who mourned for John Cohen. Once Isaac found out Orsdel was a preacher, his ideas about religion slowly began to adapt.

So on that early morning, Isaac found himself contemplating whether or not to give the church his time.

"Do you insist?" he plainly asked Orsdel.

Orsdel looked at his feet, unsure if he should laugh. "I think I do," he said, glancing at Mary.

"Alright, I'll see you on Sunday,"

"Excellent, my boy! I am forever in your debt," he rejoiced.

Isaac slumped down in his chair as Orsdel left with Mary, chatting incessantly. So far, his new surroundings had remained cold and unfamiliar. He decided to go for a ride.

Outside of the quiet cabin, the townspeople had wasted no time in beginning their daily routines. The foul gunsmith was as irritable as ever. Isaac watched as he yelled at random people walking in the street. Isaac quickly averted his gaze and walked toward the stables. Kit was gone, but Isaac noticed his mare in its stall. After getting cleaned and fed, the horse appeared completely different. Its dusty coat was now a brilliant white; as Isaac opened the stall door, it trotted elegantly toward him. *I'll call you Ruth*, he thought.

"Alright, Ruth," Isaac announced, stepping into the stirrup. "Let's see what you can do."

Isaac led her behind the stable and let her gallop through the western gulch. There weren't many structures near the gulch, only a few sheds and things of the like. Isaac rode out of the town into the hilly region that surrounded Bannack. When he hit a flat stretch of land, the mare quickened her speed. Isaac snagged his hat, the wind racing past his face.

"Heeyah!" he shouted, pressing his spurs against the horse.

In no time, he had made it to the distant mountain slope. Isaac dismounted and sat on the dirt next to a massive ash tree. On the other side of the miniature town, he could make out the path he and Mary had taken only a few days prior. He focused on the grand range of mountains that separated Bannack from Nevada City. A colossal mountain jutted out from the center of the range. As a boy, he'd seen the same peak from its opposite side and dreamed of submitting it. People always told him it was too dangerous, but he knew there must be other people who had climbed it. He'd imagine small, wintery villages sprouting in the mountain's bowl: a town of peace.

His thoughts were interrupted by a wet splash on his bare arm. A dark cloud had emerged from behind him. There was a rumble of thunder, and Ruth jerked her head up from the grass. Isaac grabbed her reins, pulled himself up, and hurried towards town.

As he passed through the western gulch once more, he noticed the deputy had resumed his post. Buck Stinson, he recalled.

"Careful out there, boy!" Buck hollered.

"Yes, Sir," Isaac shouted. He then entered the back of the stable and noticed Kit and Lucia talking near the front gate.

Isaac quietly led Ruth into her stall, when Lucia exclaimed, "There's the young gunslinger, Kit!"

Kit laughed, but Isaac said nothing. His hostility had grown ever more apparent.

"Listen, Isaac," Lucia started, more seriously this time. "Why don't you come to Skinner's tonight with me and Kit?"

Isaac turned, maintaining his bland expression. "We'll see," he muttered.

"Well there we go!" Kit yelled. "We'll see ya then."

Isaac returned to his cabin where Little John was napping. Mary was nowhere to be seen, so Isaac sat near the child and closed his eyes.

– – –

There was a loud banging on the door. Isaac didn't know how long he'd been asleep, but Little John was no longer asleep next to him. As Isaac ambled towards the door, he noticed that it was dark out.

"Yes?" he questioned at the door.

"Whatcha been doing in there, Cohen?" the unmistakable voice of Kit exclaimed.

"Minding my own business," Isaac replied, amused.

"God damnit, get out here!" Kit shouted.

Isaac opened the door to a laughing Kit. He shoved him out of the way, and they walked to the saloon diagonal of the church.

"Yever hear about the killins in this saloon?" Kit asked.

"I guess not."

"Well an old fellow, Carhart think was his name, decided to fight another gambler," Kit began. "Both of em sprayed their guns all over the place but were still standin at the end of it!"

"Huh," Isaac replied inattentively.

As they came up to the saloon, Lucia danced out of a nearby alley. "Well hello, boys," she announced with a grin. "Was beginning to think you weren't coming."

The trio walked into the crowded saloon. There was a piano blaring in the background and people grouped around gambling tables. At the bar was George Skinner. "George!" squealed Lucia. "It has just been too long!"

"Mhuh," George grunted, showing little interest.

Lucia continued her one-sided conversation, while Kit told Isaac about the Skinner brothers. A little while ago, his brother Cyrus was found hung on a tree just outside of town. No one saw the vigilante, but George went on a long hunt with no luck. Although George was never dissuaded from going on his crusade, he didn't have many supporters either. People agreed the town was better off without his brother.

Over at the bar, it appeared as though Lucia and George had taken down an entire bottle of whiskey. Lucia whispered something in George's ear, and the pair stumbled out the door.

"I didn't take Lucia for that type of girl," Isaac noted to Kit.

"She's not," Kit chuckled.

Isaac sighed. "Let's just get us some whiskey."

They strolled to the bar and stayed there for nearly an hour, telling stories and becoming more and more out of sorts. At some point, a fist fight had started at one of the gambling tables, and they decided to leave. Each holding a small bottle of liquor, the pair wobbled towards Kit's home.

Although Isaac could barely see straight, Kit's home was unexpected. It was close to the size of a shed and quite uncomfortable. Kit had a short frame, presumably to be used as a bed, and a wooden chair next to it. Kit slumped down on the frame, pulling a blanket over himself.

"Sidown, buddy!" he shrieked bizarrely.

Isaac sat on the creaking chair and within minutes was asleep.

When morning came, light poured through the slits in Kit's roof. Soon Isaac awoke in an appropriately groggy state. Kit must've already gone to the stable, because the bed was empty. Isaac crawled out of the shack and walked to the cabin. Mary was still asleep in her bed when Isaac opened the door. He grabbed some fresh clothes and went to town.

Kit's shack was closer to the stable than he'd realized last night. It sat on an elevated piece of land right above the stable. He walked over, greeted Kit, then grabbed Ruth's reins to go for a ride.

Isaac sped through the empty gulch to the rugged plain. He strayed north and followed the creek to the ridge he'd gone before.

As they slowed, Isaac calmed a panting Ruth and patted her mane. He walked her across the ridge toward the ash tree. The scenery remained the same except for a distant group of bison a little bit outside of town.

They were approaching the big tree when Isaac saw the horse. It was standing behind the ash tree's trunk but was easily discernible. Isaac thought he'd seen the horse before at the stable but wasn't sure.

Isaac jumped off Ruth and grabbed his Colt. "Hello?" he said sternly.

There was no response, so Isaac crept up to the horse. Behind it, he found Lucia working hard to string a man to the thick brand above. He quietly sat down near the trunk and watched as she struggled with the man's weight.

"So this is where you took that George fellow," Issac mused.

Lucia dropped the rope and turned around suddenly. "Damn, Isaac, no reason to sneak up on me." Lucia said.

"Uh-huh," Isaac replied, tapping his knee.

"He had it coming," Lucia muttered. "And so did that brother of his."

"So this makes you, what? Bannack's very own vigilante?" Isaac asked.

"Makes me someone that gets skeptical of recently arriving folk," she rebutted.

Isaac got up and helped her with George. As they hoisted him up the branch, Isaac realized how large of man George truly was.

After he was hanging off the ground, Lucia said, "You know, I could use someone with your–uh, *skills* on my bounties,"

"Oh yeah?" Isaac paused. "And what does that involve?"

"Not much," she explained. "Ride a bit outside town, shoot a few bad men. Kit helps too."

Isaac mounted his mare and glanced down at Lucia. "I'll see you later," he said.

Isaac rode away from the big tree, watching the eastern mountains for a distraction. That day there wasn't a cloud in the sky. He could see all the way up to the glinting peak of the tallest mountain.

After arriving back in town, he was greeted by Orsdel. "Ah, Isaac! I was looking all over for you!"

"Sorry, Brother Van, I was er–"

"Nevermind your ride! If I had a horse like that, I'd become one of those vigilante riders!" he laughed boisterously.

Isaac coughed uncomfortably. "So then, what do you need me for?"

"Well, tomorrow is our first service." Orsdel said excitedly. "And we need to make the proper arrangements."

"Right," Isaac paused. "How can I help?"

"We've got some pamphlets to post at the saloons announcing the opening of the church, and we need to grab a few chairs from George Skinner."

"Understood, I'll hand out the pamphlets," Isaac declared, wanting to avoid wherever it was George Skinner was thought to be.

Orsdel nodded joyfully and handed Isaac the pamphlets from his coat pocket. Next, Isaac made his way to the first saloon in town, near the gunsmith.

The place was pretty empty for an afternoon. It was nothing like where he'd been last night. He handed the bartender a stack of pamphlets and quickly returned to the street. The next saloon was Skinner's, which Isaac swiftly passed. There were two other saloons in town: one was near the stable and the other was amidst a sprawl of tents on the other side of the creek. Both saloons were quite bare, like the first one, except for a few drunks living out their days in disorientation.

Isaac left the last saloon and crossed the bridge back over the creek. He then returned to see if Orsdel needed any more help. To Isaac's confusion, Orsdel had managed to get the extra chairs, despite Geroge's absence. With the pews and chairs, they could support a decent sized crowd.

Kit entered the church with two poles on his back. "Oh hey there Mr. Orsdel, mind if I take Isaac out to fish the creek?"

"Hello, Kit!" Orsdel said, looking down at their progress. "Sure you can, but Isaac, be sure to be here tomorrow at dawn."

"You got it, Brother Van," Isaac yelled over his shoulder, as he and Kit rushed out of the church.

"I'm a pretty poor fisherman, Kit," Isaac said.

"Well yer in luck, Mr. Cohen, because ya happen to be with Montana's best," he proclaimed.

Isaac laughed, and they continued their hike up stream. They walked into the gulch and saw Buck Stinson sitting on his horse above them.

"Pretty boring work if you ask me," Kit whispered. "Not much of a service to the town just standin there."

Isaac's chuckle alerted Buck, who glared down at the pair. "Keep it moving, ya bastards!" he shouted, irritably.

"Useless *and* angry," Kit murmured, once they passed through the gulch. Soon, they came upon a nice deep spot in the creek; Isaac vaguely remembered this place from his morning ride. Kit placed some worm chunks on his hook and cast a line right over the deep area. By the time Isaac followed his lead, Kit already had a fish on the line. "Oh boy!" Kit shrieked. "This is one hefty son of a bitch!" He pulled the line out of the water with his bare hands, and eventually, a squirming trout emerged from the water. They placed him in the basket Kit had brought and continued fishing.

After sunset, the two of them had caught five trout. Kit had done most of the work, but Isaac still had a great time. As they walked back to town, Isaac pointed out the peak he'd noticed early that day. It was no longer highlighted by the sun but bathed in moonlight. Kit was less interested and quickly changed the subject. They talked about Lucia's bounties. Kit was indifferent to the task, but Isaac was disturbed. To almost everyone beside the two of them, Lucia was a proper school teacher. She even continued tutoring in the summer while chasing down criminals at dusk.

"You should come with us tomorrow night with that new gun of yers," Kit persuaded. "It'll give ya some more money for the family."

"Do you have a family?" Isaac interrupted.

Kit paused. "Well I suppose, somewhere," he said quietly.

"I didn't mean to–" Isaac started.

"Nope, that's alright. My momma ran off with a different man, and after that, my pa was never the same. In a year's time from then, he uh–passed. I'm lucky though; Lucia's uncle is a powerful man and gave me a place to live and some money to get me grounded."

"I'm sorry about all that, Kit," Isaac said sympathetically.

"Nah," Kit began. "Don't be, really, unless yer my momma's new man!" he laughed, until his voice became a pitiful croak.

Isaac patted his shoulder, and they talked for a little. Back in town, Kit said goodnight to Isaac and continued toward his home.

– – –

The morning came quickly. Isaac put on his finest slacks and briskly walked through the crisp air to the church. Orsdel was lighting candles in the windows when Isaac arrived.

"You truly look like your father in that attire, Isaac," Orsdel said.

Isaac looked down at his dark garb, chuckling.

"One thing is missing though," Orsdel noted. "Your father's pin, did you know of it?"

Isaac was struck by Orsdel's complete shift in disposition. The humorous preacher had become quite sincere, keeping his eyes fixed on Isaac. "Uh, no, I'm not sure if I recall that," Isaac replied. "What was it?"

"It was a small cross made of blackened steel," Orsdel paused. "It was stripped from him on the trail."

"When he was killed," Isaac stated.

"Yes, when he was killed," Orsdel looked through the window. "I traveled to Fort Benton shortly after I heard the news. Though your father's body was already on its way to Nevada City, I was able to find the doctor who examined him and ask him about the pin. You see, it was very important to him, this pin. I made it my goal to find it, but I failed."

"And that's alright," Isaac tried to affirm.

"Yes," Orsdel sighed. "Let's open the doors."

Orsdel walked over to the door while Isaac stood on the platform in the back. There was a decent crowd outside the church. All kinds of people came in, many of whom Isaac had not seen before. As the people rushed into the pews, Orsdel instantly shifted into the jubilant man Isaac was used to. Isaac wondered if any law would attend. So far in his time at Bannack, he hadn't even seen the sheriff and only met one of his deputies. Perhaps they were off on a bounty hunt, but regardless, their absence was duly noted by the lawlessness of the town at night.

"Hello, Isaac!" a voice yelled from in front of him.

Isaac looked up from the floor. In front of him Dr. Leavitt was smiling widely. "Oh hello, Doctor," Isaac returned a smile.

"Deep in thought, I see," Dr. Leavitt chuckled. "I will be sitting now, we can speak more after if you'd like."

Isaac nodded and sat in his chair behind the pulpit. Orsdel strolled up to the platform and gazed at the attendees. "Welcome, all! We are so very pleased with your attendance, and together, I'm sure we can create a proper community!"

In the back pew, Isaac noticed Mary with Little John and Kit beside her. Isaac smiled at them, and Orsdel began his sermon.

After the service, Isaac swept the dusty wooden floor and collected the hymnals from the pews. Orsdel had left with a few congregants, leaving Isaac alone in the room. Then there was a slight knock on the door and Lucia invited herself in.

"Hey, Isaac," she paused. "I forgot to say thank you earlier for the, ya know–"

"Sure," he smiled, glad to have an excuse to idle.

"Kit and I are leaving after noon. You should come with us."

"Okay," he said, looking back to the floor for blemishes. Isaac was still unsure of Lucia's vigilante endeavors, but it was better than sitting cramped in his cabin at night.

"Alright, I'll come find you when we're leaving," Lucia grinned, walking out of the church.

– – –

Later that morning, Isaac found Mary with Little John near a clearing by the creek. Although he'd been busy running around town with his new friends, Isaac noticed Mary adjusting quite well to life in Bannack.

When Isaac was near the stable, he would frequently see her reading in the apothecary. Little John was always stuck to her side wherever she went.

"Hey, Ma," Isaac said, strolling towards them.

"Hello, Isaac," Mary smiled. "Little John has missed you."

The orphan stood up awkwardly and walked towards Isaac before his knees buckled. Isaac picked him up and laughed.

"You got to be careful, little lad!" he joked.

"At first I was worried he wouldn't take to us," Mary said, gathering Little John into her arms.

"Well, you needn't worry anymore," Isaac laughed. "I won't be coming home tonight, I'm on some business for a friend."

Mary gave a quizzical look. "Alright, don't get too far away from town."

Isaac nodded and walked toward the stable where Lucia and Kit were preparing their horses. "There he is!" Kit said, placing a revolver and shotgun into his saddlebag. "You got a rope, Isaac? Sure would be nice to have one."

Isaac nodded. "How far is this bounty anyway, Lucia?" he asked.

"Well," Lucia turned from her horse. "Apparently, he's hiding at a homestead a day's ride south from here."

"And who is he again?" Kit inquired.

"One grumpy bastard," she paused. "Red Yager, that foul gunsmith."

"Damn idiot. What he do this time?" Kit said.

"Killed some folk around town."

"Wait," Isaac interrupted. "Is this the man who runs the gunshop?"

"That's him alright," Lucia replied.

Isaac drew his Colt. "He's the one who sold me this just the other day."

"Lucky you got it before his disappearance," Lucia said. "Might need it."

With that, the trio departed. This was the first time Isaac had traveled south out of Bannack. Like every ride, his attention was held by the eastern mountains. He named the tallest peak *Moriah*. They rode up and down the long stretch of hills outside Bannack until it morphed into a wide plain. Long grasses swatted at Isaac's feet while he rode. Kit's stag eventually grew tired, so they slowed. The rolling hills were still in view behind them, but just barely. There were no signs of people anywhere.

"Look," Lucia whispered, pointing at a nearby rabbit. "Might as well."

"I'll do it," Isaac said. He wanted to ensure he could still shoot well, despite not having fired his gun the past week. He sat still, watching the rabbit in the tall

47

grass. His focus was quickly disrupted by the memory of the outlaw on the road. He gritted his teeth as the image of his mother with the repeater came into his mind.

"Isaac?" Kit said, nudging him.

"Yeah okay, I'm okay."

Isaac aimed his glinting Colt at the rabbit. His eyes glanced first at the sight then at the target. He released a breath and pulled the trigger. The hammer retracted and slammed the pin, firing a bullet through the eye of the rabbit. With a quiet yelp, the rabbit was dead.

"What a shot," Kit said, wide-eyed. "Critter must've been a dozen yards out."

Lucia dismounted, grabbed the rabbit by its back legs, and threw it in her saddle bag. The group then proceeded in a swift trot. Soon a forest came into view, full of towering pines. As they moved into the woodland, the dull rambling of the wind ceased. The steps of the horses were all that could be heard. Above the trees, the sun descended into a thick blanket of clouds.

"So, Isaac," Lucia began. "Is it just you, your brother and your mother?"

"That's about all of us," Isaac answered quickly.

"Father didn't run off did he?" Kit inserted with a grin.

Isaac gave a melancholy chuckle. "He was killed on a trail south of Fort Benton."

"You know who did it?" Lucia questioned.

"Maybe a drunk. No one saw it happen." Isaac said.

"Cept those bastards who did it," Kit grunted.

"What about you, Lucia? Those dresses don't pay for themselves, do they?" Isaac asked humorously.

Lucia silently stared at him for a moment then shifted her eyes down to her horse. "I first arrived in Bannack with my uncle and his family. Uncle Sidney had been appointed as the governor of the territory, but he still made time to take care of me and teach me how to take care of myself."

Isaac was shocked. "You mean to say you're Sidney Edgerton's niece?" he questioned.

"Indeed," she said with a plain expression. "He's the one who showed me how to find certain folk who don't want to be found."

"You're telling me old Edgerton was some vigilante?" Isaac said.

"Sort of, he was a leader," she explained.

"Of the Montana Vigilantes!" Kit announced with a grin. "Guess that makes us their new crew! Lucia being related to Edgerton and all."

They all laughed. Isaac continued his inspection of the path ahead, while Kit and Lucia chatted. Eventually, they came upon a clearing with a fallen tree.

"This is as good a place as any to make camp," Isaac said, examining the empty area. He grabbed the bed rolls off Lucia's horse and set them up against the tree. Lucia grabbed some wood scraps from the forest, and Kit cooked the rabbit.

"We're probably close to the homestead," Lucia began. "We should leave before dawn."

Kit and Isaac nodded their heads in agreement, then they gathered under their blankets to wait the night out.

Rain drizzled down on them throughout the night. Isaac was too preoccupied with what the future held to sleep. Though Lucia looked at their trip as an adventure, Isaac was concerned about what Yager might attempt in defiance. He'd seen what people could do when backed into a corner.

Suddenly, Isaac heard voices and hooves approach the opposite side of the clearing. It didn't sound like a big group, but he couldn't be sure. He slowly perked his head above the log to get a look at the travelers. There were two of them. The taller one had a dark beard and rode a muscular black horse, and the other was shrouded in a long overcoat. Isaac didn't recognize either of them and quickly sunk down as they neared. Their fire had long since been extinguished, so he doubted the travelers would see them or the horses in the cover of night.

After Isaac could no longer hear their gruff voices, he woke up Kit and Lucia. "We'd better go," Isaac said. "I just saw some others on the path."

"Probably a good idea," Lucia agreed, packing her things up. "They must've been coming from the homestead. That's all this trail leads to."

Kit yawned and, with a few disapproving remarks, folded his bed roll. Soon their belongings were all packed up, and the group was moving down the path. The rain had turned into a light spray, accompanied by a low fog that descended into the forest. They couldn't see very far in front of them and had to depend on the trail for direction. A little ways down the muddy path, they found a burnt-down cottage. Inside, they scavenged a few miscellaneous cans, and Kit even found an old hunting knife and some bills.

Later, the sun rose and pierced through the crowded trees of the forest. They'd been riding for sometime now, but by Lucia's estimates, they were going to come up on the homestead soon. The forest eventually turned into a damp grassy plain. Far away, Lucia noted a distant clump of buildings.

"That oughta be the place right there," she said, her outstretched arm aiming at the homestead.

Isaac surveyed the land. Though the lowland seemed to go on for miles, there was a distinct rocky mound adjacent to the buildings. "There," he pointed. "Let's make a plan up on that hill."

The trio dismounted in the tall grasses to further obscure their approach. As they walked toward the mound, they quickly distinguished three wooden buildings on the homestead. The biggest was clearly a barn with its massive door. Right next to it was a short gray house. On its deck, there was a stubby man looking out to the fields of the farm. Near one of the fields was the last building: a small shed made of logs.

"That aint Yager," Kit said, staring at the man on the porch.

"Maybe he's inside," Isaac whispered.

They curled around the backside of the hill and tied the horses, then crawled up. From there, they could see the whole area: the buildings, the fields, and even the forest they'd come from. After much deliberation, they came up with a plan to capture Yager and waited for the sun to set.

– – –

The sun was gone, and all the lights had been extinguished except one in the house. Kit descended the hill first and crept toward his post near the barn. Isaac and Lucia came next, sneaking towards the house.

Kit prowled into the dark of the barn, revolver in hand. The walls were lined with stalls. He could hear the silent hum of the sleeping animals. He spotted a ladder leading to a loft. After glancing around the barn, he climbed the ladder.

Isaac and Lucia slowly made their way to the house's porch with their drawn guns. They approached the place the man had been standing earlier in the day. Isaac circled the house to see if he could spot anyone through the dim windows. After seeing nothing, he and Lucia crept through the front door. The planked floor was ridden with dust, and there were boxes covered in canvas scattered across the first floor. They heard creaking above them. Lucia held her finger to her lip. Isaac nodded. They tucked themselves behind the staircase, waiting for the noise to stop. But the sound was only getting louder. Through the slits of the stairs, Isaac could see the wall getting brighter and brighter until the stubby man appeared with a lantern in one hand and a knife in the other.

Isaac took a sharp breath. From this close, he could clearly make out the man's face. It bore a fierce resemblance to a different man he'd known only briefly: the man his mother had killed.

"We should get out of here," Isaac mouthed over to Lucia.

Lucia shook her head then fixed her eyes back on the man, who was almost at the stairs. He stood on the top step for a moment and looked down at the first floor.

Suddenly, the silence of the night was interrupted by a loud gunshot from the barn. The stubby man paused then raced down the stairs. Just as he'd made it to the floor, Isaac jumped up and slammed the butt of his revolver into the man's forehead. Isaac stopped for a moment to observe the heinous result of the blow but was quickly ushered out of the house by Lucia. As they ran toward the barn, they heard another shot and a faint yelp.

"Kit!" Isaac shouted into the night.

Kit shrieked, limping out of the barn door as fast as he could. Isaac grabbed Kit's arm and ran him to the back of the barn. His leg had been shot clean through. Blood was spurting out of his upper thigh.

Kit murmured, "It's him", to Isaac before passing out on the cold dirt. Lucia rushed over to his side and tied her coat around his leg. Isaac walked around the corner of the barn to see if Yager had emerged. To his bewilderment, the stubby man had stepped out of the house, knife still in hand. He locked eyes with Isaac. His crimson face twisted into a deranged smile, and then he charged, screaming a primitive cry.

In a split second, Isaac yanked out his revolver and shot the man twice, but it wasn't enough to stop him. When the man veered his knife toward Isaac, Isaac swiftly countered with the barrel of his revolver. Using his other hand, the man punched Isaac in the face then kicked him square in the ribs while he was down. The man paused in a lethargic state, and Isaac frantically crawled toward the house.

He looked behind his right and saw the man on the ground, likely dead. When he looked to his left, he saw none other than Red Yager. After Yager saw Isaac, he sprinted toward him and stepped on his neck. Isaac tried to call out for Lucia, but no sound came out.

"Hmm, who do we have here?" Yager hissed, crouching down to Isaac. "Wait, I know you! Yer that new Cohen fella in town! Why'd ya have to go straight for my bounty? We coulda been friends ya know! I guess you Cohen's just don't like to have friends... Yer daddy sure didn't."

Isaac glared. He struggled with a new rage and looked up at Yager with utter contempt. Yager laughed, pointing a gun at Isaac, "And now yull die as he did."

Out of nowhere, a rope flew out over them and snagged Yager backward by the torso. His wielding hand was instantly blown off by the shotgun Lucia was holding, while a kneeling Kit held the lasso taught. Isaac watched in exhaustion as they tied Yager up and placed a sack over his head.

Despite the late hour, Lucia and Isaac decided to leave right away. Kit needed a doctor for the gun wounds in his leg, and Yager had to be delivered before he would die from his own injury. After blowing off Yager's right hand and tying him up, Lucia had put an old dirty glove from the barn onto his stump. Yager was then stowed on the back of Isaac's horse. He didn't say much throughout his capture. The only hint of his life was the occasional deep breath.

If Yager so much as yawned, Isaac would twist around and smack his head with the Colt. Isaac was desperate to let his anger out. Yager's weak acknowledgment of his father's murder was ingrained in his memory. He couldn't believe he'd shown Yager a basic level of pleasantry in the gun shop.

Shortly after Yager had been tied up, Isaac told Lucia and Kit what Yager had said. Lucia tried her hardest to diffuse the situation so as to not kill their bounty before they made it back to Bannack. Kit even said the sheriff might let Isaac kill him. But Isaac was livid. He had been angrily pacing around the barn before they departed.

As they made their way to the forest's opening, Kit began to slump against the neck of his horse. "You alright there, Kit?" Isaac asked, trotting up to him.

"Mmm," Kit groaned.

Isaac glanced over at Lucia, unsure of what to say. "We'll be home soon," he asserted.

Their trip through the forest was not as quiet as before. The horses' hooves clapped loudly due to the pace, while the injured gripped from pain. The mood, however, was lifted as the sun rose. The light poured through the canopy, gleaming down on them. Soon, they had slipped through the final trees of the forest and were riding into the brilliant field. Isaac pulled his Colt out from his saddle. Its metallic glow was now obscured by dried blood. He was numb from the interaction of his anger and regret. Yager's companion was the first man he'd killed: a barely-armed man at that. But, Isaac quickly learned to accept the justification of the man's knife. Supposing they'd swapped places, Isaac was sure he'd have been gunned down just as fast.

"Stop for a minute," Lucia said, looking toward Kit's sunken body. "Let's get him off the horse."

"Alright, but only a minute," Isaac replied, glancing up to the sun.

Together, they pulled Kit from his horse down to the thick grass. Isaac untied the cloth on Kit's leg, revealing his oozing thigh. "Goddamnit, Cohen! Watch yer fingers!" Kit cried.

"Right, sorry. We need to stop the bleeding."

Lucia looked around them. "Isaac, I need you to find a stick or two, dry ones. Seeing as you boys didn't bring any bandages, we're going to have to do this the way Dr. Leavitt would."

Isaac sprung up and searched the field for sticks. He grabbed a clump of dead grass and picked up some small sticks beside them. Lucia rubbed the sticks over the grass until a small flame appeared. She then pulled out the shotgun from Kit's saddle and held the barrel above the fire.

"No, Lucia, you don't mean to–?" Kit said.

"I do. You're going to need to trust me. Dr. Leavitt showed me how last month."

As the fire grew, the barrel warmed. Eventually the gun was almost too hot to hold, so Lucia scooted toward Kit. "It'll only hurt a bit," she promised.

Isaac sat behind Kit, holding his arms back. Lucia pressed the steaming metal onto Kit's thigh. He screamed in pain, his face grimacing. Lucia lifted the gun and kicked the fire out. "There you are," she grinned; the red skin around the wound had darkened to a crude brown. "I wonder if Yager'll die from his own bleeding or from a hanging?" Lucia pondered, looking over at their stowed bounty.

"Maybe neither," Isaac muttered, helping Kit up.

"Hey," Lucia began. "Money first, then execution. Got it?"

Isaac walked over to Ruth and bashed Yager's hood. The man grumbled. "Got it," Isaac smirked.

The rest of the ride to Bannack was uneventful. Kit was upright on his horse again, and Lucia was happy with their arrest. Isaac was getting back to his usual self but was still very aware of what Yager had done. He wondered why his father had been the target of Yager's gun. Like most young boys, Isaac had idolized his father. But even as he got older, he could find no fault with his father. Everything John Cohen did seemed to fit some altruistic motive. Isaac knew he was missing something, but he couldn't figure out what it was. Yager wouldn't have remembered the name of some incidental road kill. Yager must have known his father: but how?

They were halfway through the hillscape when they started to see Bannack's sprawl of life. The wind had picked up, and the sun was at the horizon once more. The line of hills to the east had elevated into the great ridge. Isaac could see Moriah in the center. Its peak was as vivid as ever; the setting sun bathed the mountain in an orange glow.

Within the hour, they descended through the gulch to the stable. The horses were weary and just about collapsed at their stalls.

"Get off," Isaac commanded Yager.

"Heh," Yager wheezed. He slid off Ruth's back, landing on his side with a groan.

"Help him up," Lucia said to Isaac. "We need to show the deputy he's living." She turned to Kit. "And you need to get to Leavitt's."

Kit agreed and left with the help of a passerby. Isaac snatched the man's arm. Once Yager was on his feet, Isaac pushed him toward the street. They walked toward the sheriff's office while Lucia unsaddled the horses.

Isaac dragged Yager with the rope he was bound by. The townspeople stared as the pair came down the street. Both of their clothes were stained with blood and muck. At the front end of the street, Isaac noticed there was a light on in the sheriff's office and quickened his pace. As he approached, he noticed two familiar horses hitched on the side of the office.

Isaac marched up to the door. Inside, he heard hushed voices talking. Isaac quickly knocked during a silence. There was a sudden rummaging, and someone said, "Come in."

Isaac pushed open the creaking door, pulling Yager in after him. There were two men inside. The one at the desk had slicked back haircut and a thick beard, and the other had a mop of light brown hair.

"Evening," the man at the desk said. "Who might you be, son?"

"Isaac Cohen. Came here only a short while ago with my mother," Isaac said.

The sheriff's lip twitched. "Well, Isaac Cohen, I'm Henry Plummer, the Sheriff around these parts," he paused, shifting his eyes to Yager. "He for me?"

"I suppose, yes. I'm here to collect his bounty."

Plummer grabbed a few bills from his desk and placed them near Isaac. Yager scoffed as Isaac collected the reward.

Before Isaac walked out of the door, he turned and asked, "Could I do the hanging, Sheriff? It did say he was wanted for *murder* did it not?"

Plummer hesitated, looking at Yager's sagging glove. "Even if we kill him, it doesn't give you the right," he clarified. "But I'll see what I can do."

Early next morning, Isaac made his way to Kit's shack above the stable. He was eager to see how his friend was doing, but even after several knocks, there was no answer. Isaac thought it'd be a good idea to check Dr. Leavitt's shop. He strolled down a path to the street. There were only a few people up at this hour. Most of them were workers, preparing for a long day of mining. He spotted Orsdel on the steps of the church with a book in his hands and walked up to him.

"Brother Van!" Isaac greeted.

"Oh hello, Isaac," Orsdel said, glancing at the street.

"How are things with the church?" Isaac asked.

"You know," Orsdel said quietly, shifting closer to Isaac. "You shouldn't be getting mixed up with vigilante business. Lots of people saw you in the street. It could make you a target."

Isaac gave a slight frown. "What?"

"I'm just saying. That life is a dangerous one. People here don't take too kindly to road agents. Your father–" Orsdel looked down. "Your father wouldn't want this."

"It was one job," Isaac affirmed sternly. "I'll see you on Sunday."

With that, Isaac paced away toward the apothecary. He wiped the irritated look off his face and peered through the window. All the carefully ordered glass sat motionless. Isaac opened the door and began examining the various tonics on the wall nearest to him. Through the reflection, he saw Dr. Leavitt descend the back stairs.

"Morning, Doctor."

Dr. Leavitt jumped. "Lord, Isaac! Eager lad aren't you?" he laughed.

"Sorry, Sir, I was just wondering if Kit was here."

"Ahh, of course! You came to the right place. He's just up those stairs, second room on the left."

Isaac walked toward the stairs. "How is he?"

Dr. Leavitt hesitated, unsure of whether or not to mention Kit's suspected saturnism. "He's... alright. Quick thinking on the lady's part to cauterize the wound, however, he did still have a bullet inside."

Isaac looked away from the doctor.

"Don't worry. He'll live, but next time, try not to shoot each other when you're hunting for pelts! He's very lucky the bullet didn't hit his middle thigh."

"Won't forget, Sir." Isaac chuckled to himself and continued up the steps. The wood floor creaked as he walked to Kit's door.

"Kit?" Isaac asked, slowly pushing open the door.

"Yeah," Kit murmured, lying in a bed across the room with a bottle to his chest.

"Are you alright?" Isaac questioned, looking at the new red cloth on Kit's leg.

"Think so?" Kit replied. "The whiskey is... helpin."

"Next time we ought to be more careful *hunting for pelts*," Isaac grinned.

Kit just nodded, unable to laugh at the weak alibi. His brown hair was taped to his sweaty forehead, eyes twitching aggressively. Isaac sat there for a while, until Kit fell into an awkward slumber. Despite Leavitt's reassurances, he was still worried for Kit. It all seemed like a dream. He had never worked under the law in all his years at Nevada City. But Bannack wasn't Nevada City. In Bannack, the street wasn't safe at night. In Bannack, outlaws flooded into town to escape higher law. With the endless list of criminal acts, it seemed normal folk either became ignorant or became enforcers. Isaac didn't know if he'd completely chosen his side. His father had avoided outlaws, and it had gotten him killed. But when Isaac had seeked outlaws, his friend had been shot and his reputation injured.

Isaac said farewell to Kit and descended the stairs to the apothecary. There were a few people ruffling through various items in the corner, and Dr. Leavitt was organizing something at his counter.

"Thank you, Doctor."

Dr. Leavitt looked up. "Of course, Isaac! Please come back at any time!"

"Do you know where Lucia is?" Isaac asked at the door.

"She has been quite mysterious lately, but maybe she's tutoring? I would check the schoolhouse," Dr. Leavitt answered with a smile.

Isaac nodded and left. The schoolhouse stood near the center of the main street, diagonal to the church. It was a tall white building with five big windows in the front. Isaac brushed open the door. Lucia sat near the back wall with three students sitting in front of her. The wide array of desks suggested a large class during the school year.

"Isaac!" Lucia said, getting up from her chair. She turned to the children. "Kids," she announced. "This is Mr. Cohen, a friend of mine."

The children awkwardly waved to Isaac as he greeted them with a chuckle.

"So what brings you here, Mr. Cohen?"

"Well," he began, looking at the staring students. "I was just... saying hello! I hope the rest of the lesson goes well."

Lucia laughed. "If you're interested in saying hello again, our session will be done in a quarter hour. You can come by then."

"Alright!" Isaac said, turning his red face to the door. Outside, he sat on an old bench and gazed at the passersby. Just then, he saw the sheriff walking down the road with his deputies. They seemed to be in the middle of a debate when the sheriff stepped aside to speak with Isaac.

"Sheriff," Isaac nodded.

"Just the man I was looking for," Plummer declared. "I'll permit your request, on one condition."

"Thank you, Sir," Isaac grinned. "What is the condition?"

"You see, the deputies and I were wondering what kind of basis you have to be the one to hang him. A personal vendetta perhaps?"

"Well, I have reason to believe he killed my father on the road from Fort Benton. I'd like to avenge my father's death."

Plummer's brooding expression gradually shifted to a smile. "As good a reason as any," Plummer agreed. "We'll have to postpone the hanging until our jails are emptied of their current occupants, but I'll summon you when the time comes."

The timing wasn't ideal for Isaac, but nothing could spoil his mood. He continued to sit on the bench until Lucia and her students rushed out of the schoolhouse.

"What'd he have to say?" Lucia said under her breath as her students scattered.

"I can hang him," Isaac explained. "When the jails are empty."

Lucia scoffed. "I don't think the jails are ever empty."

"Look," Isaac pointed to the rocky hill adjacent to Bannack. "They're growing emptier by the minute." Sheriff Plummer stood on a hanging platform, holding a man by his arm. A small crowd had gathered near the base of the platform as the man gave his last, inaudible words.

"Huh," Lucia thought. "I suppose you're right."

"Do you want to go for a ride?" Isaac asked.

"Where to?"

"The hanging tree?"

Lucia laughed. "Alright, Cohen. Let's go."

They headed to the stable. Inside it seemed empty without Kit's bright demeanor. Lucia carefully untied her brown horse and Isaac his mare. Isaac saddled up and

68

raced out through the gulch, looking over his shoulder at Lucia. She grinned and clapped her horse's ribs with her boots. Isaac faced forward and spotted the big ash tree in the distance. From just outside town, the tree appeared like a speck of dust suspended on the horizon. They galloped across the hills, bathed in the afternoon sunlight. Lucia was dashing up to Isaac when he slowed to give Ruth a break.

"Do I win then?" she joked.

Isaac smiled and trotted up to the tree. The rope that had once held George Skinner had been cut a few feet up. Isaac hitched Ruth to the tree and sat down as Lucia strolled toward him. Since the tree was a ways up the slope of the ridge, they could see almost the entire plain they'd rode through. Past the plain they spotted a bit of the town, and past that stood the eastern mountain range. Moriah was concealed in a dense clump of clouds. Isaac could barely make out the base of the great mountain.

"Have you ever seen that tall peak east of Bannack?" he inquired.

"Sure I have," she replied. "Hard to miss."

"Has anyone in town ever been up there?"

"Back when my uncle was the governor, he led an expedition up there for some odd reason. Probably had to do with the Montana Vigilantes," she explained. "But I haven't seen anyone up there since."

69

Isaac maintained his gaze at the ridge while Lucia leaned against the tree and began to whittle a small chunk of wood. The silence was filled by a swift wind that rustled the branches above them. Isaac looked up at her. Her light brown hair swayed in the wind.

"What's that going to be?" Isaac asked, pointing at the piece of wood she was carving.

She bit her lip. "What do you want it to be?"

"I'm not sure," he paused. "My father used to whittle." Isaac sighed and began picking the grass next to his legs.

"He'd be proud of what you've done with Yager," she said. "Merciless bastard."

Isaac nodded and suggested they get a move on as the sun was getting low. Lucia pulled Isaac's arm to usher him up, and they both mounted their horses. The horses galloped down the slope toward the plain. Soon they were riding through the hills with the wind of their backs. Lucia looked over at Isaac to say something, but his eyes were fixed on Moriah's hazey peak. They entered town and stabled the horses without much more conversation. Isaac then walked to his cabin and went to sleep.

The next day, Isaac decided to go to the church and see if Orsdel needed help for the next day's service. When Isaac left the cabin, he felt a cold wind brush against his face and glanced at a gray sky. He put his hand on the backdoor of the church but paused. Inside, he heard a soft voice singing to a piano's unsettling melody:

"On a hill far away stood an old rugged cross
The emblem of suffering and shame
And I love that old cross where the dearest and best
For a world of lost sinners was slain"

Isaac knocked twice at the end of the verse and was greeted by Orsdel's jovial voice. "Hello, Isaac!" he exclaimed. "I was just about to go see if you were available."

"Brother Van," Isaac nodded. "What is it you need help with?"

"Well, I was more so seeking an audience. But perhaps you could sweep while I talk."

Isaac picked up the broom and turned towards Orsdel. "If this is about my bounty hunt, save me the preaching for Sunday."

"No," Orsdel smiled. "It is just a story."

"So long as it doesn't involve Yager," Isaac said, beginning to sweep.

"I met a man once in Ohio. He was as bloodthirsty as men came. During the war, we fought alongside each other in the cavalry. He was always the first one to charge toward the graybacks. He was a true soldier: loyal, fearless, and ruthless. He'd plunge his sword into each corpse on the battlefield to ensure their demise. But he was also a good man. Outside of fighting, he was different. He once made me stop with him at a widow's house, so we could fix her tattered roof. You see, Isaac, this man had the instincts of a predator, but the will of a saint. He never killed for the thrill of it; he killed out of some intense sense of duty. After the war, he didn't carry a gun on him. In fact, he gave his weapon to his son. And where he used to store extra bullets on his shirt, he pinned a shiny black cross."

Isaac looked up from his sweeping, now understanding who the characters in the story were.

"Isaac," Orsdel continued. "All I'm asking is for you to honor your father's legacy. Kill when you must. I can understand Yager, but none else. Some people deserve to die, but if we all killed out of passion, there wouldn't be anyone left to bury the dead."

Isaac sat in the pew next to him and stared at the dusty floor. A minute passed.

"Do you understand?" Orsdel asked.

"Yes," Isaac said, standing up. "But I haven't fought my war yet."

Orsdel sighed. "You might be right, but remember the principle."

Isaac gave a slight nod and continued sweeping. Orsdel turned toward the piano and began playing again:

"So I'll cherish the old rugged cross
Till my trophies I at last lay down
I will cling to the old rugged cross
And exchange it someday for a crown"

Isaac placed his broom down and clapped. Orsdel stooped into a comical bow, making Isaac chuckle. "You've got quite a talent for that," Isaac commented. "Maybe you can teach me sometime."

Orsdel grinned. "I'd be glad to."

They continued a pleasant conversation until they were disrupted by a soft knock on the front door.

"Isaac? Mr. Orsdel?" Lucia called out.

Isaac jogged to the door and opened it. "What's going on?"

"It's Kit. He's gotten worse," she said. Orsdel got up from the piano, and all three of them rushed across the street to the apothecary.

"Kit?" Isaac called, opening his door. Isaac first saw Dr. Leavitt's black coat. The doctor was hunched over Kit's bed with his glasses at the tip of his nose. Kit looked like a clammy corpse. His face was pale and his eyes sullen. His chest rose and fell rapidly.

Orsdel began whispering a prayer in the corner while Lucia sat next to the bed with Dr. Leavitt. "What can you do?" Lucia asked Leavitt quietly.

"It appears–" he paused. "Well it's really no fault of yours, but the wound seems to have taken the cautery poorly."

Dr. Leavitt then pulled back Kit's sheet, revealing his grisly thigh. There was thick, yellow liquid leaking from the wound. Lucia gasped and looked as though she would cry. But instead, she stood up and embraced Isaac. He staggered for a moment then hugged her back as they watched Dr. Leavitt poke at the wound. After Orsdel left, they sat on the window sill and observed Dr. Leavitt's treatment of Kit.

Dr. Leavitt forced a gulp of quinine into Kit, followed by a shot of whiskey. After grabbing a jar from the first floor, he shifted his attention toward Kit's leg. He used a small blade to cut through the wound. A mixture of blood and the yellow liquid came running out of the laceration. Dr. Leavitt quickly placed the jar next to Kit's thigh to collect the residue.

Isaac closed his eyes while Kit moaned in discomfort. The liquid was growing ever more red, and Isaac couldn't help but think further leakage was unnecessary. "Can't we stop for now and see if any more sleep might help him, Doctor?" Isaac suggested.

"We must drain the wound to rid him of this illness," Dr. Leavitt asserted.

Lucia stood up and walked over to Kit. "We can continue draining tomorrow if he's not better, Dr. Leavitt," Lucia said firmly. "If he dies, it'll be on my hands, not yours."

Dr. Leavitt nodded solemnly and left once more to find his sewing supplies. Kit gave a meager nod towards Lucia and Isaac before closing his eyes. Isaac looked out through the window behind him. He saw his mother and Little John sitting on the church steps. Down the road, he saw the sheriff talking to a few men on horses. Isaac's gaze was interrupted when Dr. Leavitt returned to the room with his bag.

"Try not to stir," Dr. Leavitt encouraged. He then pulled out an old needle and began threading it through the flaps of skin adjacent to the wound.

After the procedure was completed, Kit sat up on the bed. His dazed eyes shuddered at the exercise. He feebly gave an expression of gratitude, and Isaac and Lucia made their way downstairs. The first floor was empty except for the dull hum of the wind through the door.

"I'd better go," Lucia said. "I promised to help one of my students with her ciphering this afternoon."

Isaac nodded and followed Lucia through the door. "Good luck!" he yelled as she walked toward the schoolhouse. A little girl ran up to her right as she turned to reply. Lucia gave a cheery shrug toward Isaac and continued down the road.

Isaac's eyes shifted to the sheriff, who had passed Lucia and was now headed for him. Isaac stood up on the apothecary's porch as Plummer approached him. "This afternoon you'll hang him," he announced. "The town's going to be better off without that pest." He spat at the dusty ground and walked away before Isaac could speak. Isaac paused before stepping off the porch and strolled to Mary and Little John at the church.

"You mind telling me what this talk of bounty hunting is all about?" Mary inquired firmly.

"It's the man, Ma," Isaac explained, glancing down at Little John. "He murdered Pa."

Mary gazed silently at the street for a moment then looked back at Isaac. She laughed bleakley and picked up Little John. After giving Isaac a cold embrace, she strode toward the cabin.

Isaac stood up on the lonely church steps. He slowly walked around the church to the shiny creek, where he sat down on the hard bank. The cold water flowed quickly past his shoes. Across from Isaac there was a man wading into the water. He held a rusty pan in his hand. To maintain his balance in the current, he stretched his other arm out above the water. Isaac met the man's gaze, and they exchanged a nod. The man leaned into the water and began ruffling with the creek's rocky floor. Next, he deposited samples of the dirt into his pan and dipped it in the water. Isaac watched this process for the rest of the hour, seeing no reason to be anywhere else. Each time the man would lift the pan out of the water, gold specs appeared on what was otherwise a plate of dull rocks.

Later, the man climbed out of the creek and packed up his things. He hastily left his claim and crossed the bridge over to town. Just as Isaac refocused on the running water, the man appeared beside him.

"You want a drink, son?" the man grinned. Isaac could now make out the worn features of his face. His nose was crooked and his hair a dark gray.

"Sure," Isaac replied.

The two of them walked toward the stable until the man ushered him into a saloon. Isaac vaguely remembered the saloon from delivering Orsdel's pamphlets. The man sat at a corner table next to the door and gestured to the chair in front of him. The barkeeper placed two shots of whiskey on the table before Isaac even sat down.

"The name's Wyatt," the man said cordially, sipping his glass.

"I'm Isaac, Isaac Cohen."

"Good to meet you, Isaac," Wyatt grinned. "Have you ever tried your hand at panning?"

"I guess I never have, sir. My father always seemed to have a quarrel with gold."

"What a shame," Wyatt joked. "If he ever has a change of heart, you let me know."

Isaac chuckled. "You have a family?" he asked.

Wyatt looked at the small glass in front of him. "Yeah, I do. Not what it once was, though," he said somberly. "But that's family."

"I know all too well," Isaac agreed.

"Was it that father of yours?" Wyatt inquired, glancing up to Isaac.

"Yes it w–" Isaac started. "How'd you know that?"

"Bannack aint a place for men with gold quarrels," Wyatt smiled. "My regards for your father."

"Thanks I suppose," Isaac said. "You lose someone, too?"

"Yeah. My boy. He could have been your age when he passed," Wyatt paused, drinking the rest of his whiskey. "Hard to remember all these years later."

A hard knock on the window captured Isaac's attention. Henry Plummer stood outside the saloon. He signaled for Isaac to come out with one hand.

"I've got to take care of something," Isaac told Wyatt. "I'll be back."

Wyatt nodded as Isaac got up and exited. Isaac ran out the door and greeted Plummer. On the sheriff's dark coat, he seemed to have a new piece in addition to his metal badge. Before Isaac could see it any closer, Plummer rode off toward the hanging hill.

Isaac ran to the stable to mount Ruth. A warm wind accompanied him as he rode down the street. After passing the gunshop on the other side of town, he broke from the trail and headed for the hill next to town. The hill was covered in big rocks and sage. Towards the top, the terrain began to flatten. That's when Isaac saw the hanging platform and the crowd surrounding it. The wooden beams perfectly framed Moriah, which stood far behind it.

Approaching the group of townsfolk near the platform, Isaac realized he may well have been the last one to arrive. Orsdel and Mary sat on a boulder a decent distance from the crowd. Lucia was lurking on the edge of the crowd, apparently looking for Isaac. There were many others that Isaac did not know; most of them were cursing at Yager, who was slouched in front of the platform.

"Cohen!" Plummer shouted from the platform. "We don't have all day! Get up here!"

Isaac rode past the standing crowd right up to the sheriff. His deputies sulked on the sides of the platform as Isaac dismounted and climbed up. Isaac saw all the eager eyes in the crowd focus on him. Deputy Ned Ray seized

Yager's arm and forced him up the steps. The mob applauded as Yager was fixed in the noose.

"Quiet down!" Plummer yelled to the crowd. "Red Yager! You are charged with the murder of the Smith family and of being a member of the notorious Innocents gang." Plummer then turned to Yager and asked, "Any last words, Red?"

Yager grinned in amusement. "Ya know, I've done a lot of bad in my life. I've robbed, raped, and killed." He glanced at Plummer. "Thank God for this sheriff and his glorious pursuit of justice. Where would we be without him? And who can forget his new vigilante Mr. Cohen! By the way Cohen," Yager said, shifting his head to be able to look at Isaac. "I'm real sorry about yer father. Though ya may get pleasure from killing me, it won't be vengeance. Only one person can give ya that," Yager laughed, now looking straight at Plummer.

Isaac looked at Plummer, too. His face was stained with a mixture of disgust and anger. That's when Isaac noticed the nature of the metal piece next to Plummer's badge. The glinting pin on his chest: it was a cross. It was *the* cross.

Yager continued, his eyes fixed on the sheriff, "The Innocents aint what we used to be, Henry. We're more like a pack of dogs now." Yager tilted his head back down to the crowd. "So ya know folks, your sheriff, he's our *leader*." The townsfolk gasped and murmured in low voices. Yager chuckled. "A big surprise I see? Well—"

"Enough of this!" Plummer screamed. He frantically drew his blackened revolver and shot Yager dead. Isaac could only watch as the mob turned their sights on the sheriff and his deputies. Isaac stood just feet away from Yager's gruesome corpse: his body swung from the untouched noose. Isaac's thoughts were disrupted by the loud roar of another revolver. An old man from the crowd started firing at the platform.

"You crooked bastards!" the old man shrieked. He fired two misplaced shots before Buck Stinson pulled up his repeater and killed the man.

"You dare question the law!" another man erupted, shooting his gun toward the old man's corpse.

"ORDER!" Plummer shouted, shooting several rounds toward the sky. "If anybody pulls out a gun, they die!" Ned and Buck were now at the sheriff's side, pointing their weapons wildly at the crowd. But it was no use, the clash had begun. Isaac remained next to the deputies, his eyes fixed to the black cross on Plummer's shirt. Something was building inside of him: his breathing quickened; he felt an uneasy sensation in his stomach; his forehead burned. Ned, who was the closest to Isaac, turned his head to see where the heavy breathing was coming from. Isaac bit down hard in an attempt to stifle his growing passion.

"Calm, boy," Ned muttered to Isaac, turning his head back to the bewildered mob.

"Hey," Isaac called to Ned.

"What did I–" as Ned turned his head, Isaac quickly removed his Colt from his waistband and struck Ned in the jaw. The deputy screamed, and Isaac aimed down and shot him in the foot. Buck and Plummer turned to figure the commotion. Buck jumped over to Ned and tackled Isaac to the floor. Plummer took cover behind the platform and started firing shots into the crowd.

"I'll see you in hell, boy!" Buck seethed, grasping Isaac's gun from the floor. Isaac gritted his teeth, hoping that he'd see his father in whatever place the fatal bullet may take him. But before Buck could pull the trigger, Orsdel appeared with Lucia at his side. Orsdel pulled the deputy off of Isaac, and Lucia helped him descend the platform.

"We have to get out of here," Lucia urged. Isaac nodded gravely. They raced to Mary, who was panicked from all the gunfire.

"Let's go, Ma!" Isaac yelled, mounting Ruth. As Mary got up, Isaac looked over to the platform to see what was happening. Orsdel hadn't escaped. He was taking blows from Buck in front of the scrambling crowd.

Both men were bloodied and tiring. Orsdel had miraculously got a hold on Buck around his neck. He squeezed his arm around Buck's neck with all his might. Buck closed his eyes, unable to breathe any longer. Then there was a distinct gunshot, and Orsdel fell to the ground. Plummer emerged from behind the platform, his revolver still aimed at Orsdel.

"ORSDEL!" Isaac cried, trying to maneuver the horse back. By the time Isaac got a hold on the reins, Lucia had already directed the mare toward town with a slap to its rear. Lucia then jumped onto her own horse with Mary and followed Isaac to town. The three of them raced to the cabin. Behind them, the hill had turned into a battleground; neighbors turned on neighbors. The sheriff and his deputies fired randomly into the mob as women and children fled the scene.

Isaac's face was covered in wet streaks by the time they arrived at the cabin. Mary jumped off of Lucia's horse and quickly began collecting their belongings from inside. Little John abruptly woke up from his peaceful nap amidst the chaos.

"I need to warn Kit," Lucia told Isaac.

"He can't leave. It's no use," Isaac replied quietly. With a defiant shake of the head, Lucia ran to the apothecary. Isaac turned to help Mary collect as many of their belongings as they could. He heard Plummer howl with devilish laughter amongst the shrieking townsfolk. Plummer was just visible from their cabin, his black attire flowing in the wind. He was now flanked by a small militia of his followers. Mary came out of the cabin with a crate full of goods. Little John was sitting calmly inside the crate. Isaac scrambled onto his mare and pulled Mary up with him. Then, they rushed to the apothecary to find Lucia.

The apothecary door was still open when they arrived. Lucia's horse idled outside. Isaac jumped off of Ruth and ran up the stairs. Dr. Leavitt leaned against a wall in the hallway, gazing through the window.

"You should be gone," he warned, keeping his eye on the hill. "They're almost here."

"What about you, Doctor? What about Kit?" Isaac pressed.

"A cripple and an old man? That's a crime even to criminals," Dr. Leavitt affirmed.

"Fine," Isaac muttered, rushing into Kit's room. "Lucia, we—"

Lucia was sitting down on Kit's bed. She held his hand as he shouted for them to leave. "Out with ya!" Kit cried. "Think of yer families!" Isaac gave Kit a firm embrace and tugged on Lucia's arm.

"We have to leave," Isaac pleaded. Lucia reluctantly stood up and left with Isaac. Outside the store,

Mary was anxiously waiting. At the opposite end of the road, the gang had appeared. Four masked men, the two deputies, and the sheriff all watched from a distance as Isaac struggled to escape.

"The Innocents will find you, boy!" Plummer screamed. Once mounted, Isaac hammered his heel into Ruth, and they rode off toward the southern forest.

– – –

By the time they reached the woods, Isaac was finally sure they weren't being followed. Little John might've been the most composed of the group during the ride. Mary had been sobbing for Orsdel, while Isaac and Lucia put on brave faces. Isaac wanted to curse his mother for moving to Bannack in the first place.

Isaac quickly realized where Lucia was leading them; the path was just as it was a week ago. They came upon a familiar clearing and took a rest. Isaac was replaying the events through his head: Yager's final words, Plummer's cross, Orsdel's sacrifice. He couldn't believe he hadn't seen this coming. Hate towards one had blinded him to the reality of another. With his lamentation came a controlled fury. A single ambition formed in his vehement mind: kill the devil.

86

It took another day of riding before they reached the homestead. The grim sky cast a long shadow on the farm as they neared. Lucia climbed off her horse to scout out the area. Beside the gently flowing grasses on the perimeter, everything on the homestead seemed perfectly still. Lucia crept up behind the barn and looked around the corner to the house. She gave a gesture for Isaac to come to her.

"The dead man's body is still over there," she said, nodding toward the house. "Must be abandoned."

"Alright," Isaac replied. "I'll grab the horses—"

"Wait. We ought to move the body for Mary and Little John's sake, don't you think?"

Isaac nodded lifelessly and walked around the barn. On the other side, he saw the muddy stage of his execution. He quickly spotted the stubby man near the house. The dead man's stench was rancid. His pale flesh was rotting all over. Isaac took the man's arm and pulled him toward the back of the house. This man's weight surprised Isaac. He bent his knees and dragged the body with all his might. On the backside of the house, Isaac saw a long feeding trough. He hauled the man's legs into the trough first, then he slowly pulled the rest of him in.

When Isaac came around to the front of the house, Mary and Lucia were there waiting. "Everything looks good around here," Isaac announced, glancing at Lucia.

"We'd better go inside," Lucia said. "Can't be sure they didn't send a tracker."

"There's a plan," Isaac said, stepping onto the creaking porch. He opened the door and entered. Lucia and Mary followed him in. Covering the floor were the canvas crates they had noted before. Isaac pulled the canvas sheet off one of them. There were a dozen revolvers in the crate. He began stripping all the crates around him, finding more weapons, canned rations, and a hunk of dynamite.

"This isn't just a farm," Lucia remarked. "It's a hideout."

"Guess that explains why Yager was here," Isaac added.

Mary gave Isaac a look of distaste and started rummaging through the box of rations. "I'll fashion us all something warm to eat," she said quietly. "It's been a long day."

After Mary left with Little John, Lucia began searching through the remaining crates. She collected the ammunition at the bottom of each crate and tested the condition of the weapons. One crate was full of polished repeaters that appeared relatively new. Lucia held the rifle up to her eyes and inspected the lever. The word *Winchester* was engraved across the wooden body.

"I've seen a man take out ten people at once with one of these," she commented.

Isaac, who had been fiddling with his revolver, glanced over. "You should take it. I might need a new gun as well," he said, raising the crooked barrel of his Colt. "Ruth jumped on it in the commotion."

"That's a real shame," Lucia said. "Pretty hard to get another one of those out here."

"I never learned how to shoot a rifle right," Isaac mentioned, picking up one of the repeaters.

"Let's go outside," Lucia responded. "I can give you a few words of advice." Isaac followed Lucia out the door. They walked toward the open farmland in search of a good shooting area. Lucia leaned her rifle on a nearby post then set up a skinny log a dozen yards from Isaac. He unslung the rifle from his shoulder and pointed it toward the sky.

"You might want to back away from that target a little," Isaac noted. Lucia ran back toward him and watched him aim toward the log. Isaac cocked the lever, matching the iron sight to the target.

"Now the target might be a little–" Lucia started but was interrupted by the roar of the gunshot. Isaac's shot collided with the top of the thin log, making it fall to the ground instantly. "Nice shooting," Lucia said, staring at the fallen target. She then picked up her own repeater and focused on the log. With only a few seconds of aiming, she released a shot that hit the center of the wooden target.

"Scarecrow?" Isaac said, pointing to a post behind the log.

Lucia smiled and agreed to the competition. "Go!" Lucia yelled. She pulled her repeater up to her eye and let loose another shot. A split second later, Isaac's own gun fired, sending a bullet straight at the scarecrow. Both the bullets passed through the hay body of the scarecrow.

"Metal bin!" Isaac shouted, turning to focus on the water bin next to the house. He hit the target with a *clang*, just as Lucia fired.

"Huh, not much of a beginner now, are you?" Lucia commented. "Let's go for that barn lantern."

"That's pretty far," Isaac said, trying to focus his sights on the lantern. Lucia already had a steady angle on the target, and within a minute, she fired a shot toward the barn. The bullet cracked into the barn's wooden wall, missing the lantern.

"How did–" Lucia began. "You're never going to hit that."

"The wind," Isaac answered. He angled his repeater slightly up and to the right of the lantern. After a few breaths, he pulled the trigger and shattered the lantern's glass. Isaac looked over to Lucia, who was already heading inside.

"Whatever," she said. "Let's eat."

Inside the house, Mary was heating up some canned food over the furnace. Little John was sitting on the ground, playing with a small wooden ball. Lucia and Isaac returned their repeaters to the crate and sat at the table near Mary.

"Were you two firing those guns?" Mary asked harshly. "Chances are they sent someone to ensure we wouldn't be coming back to Bannack with trouble, and you two could be leading them right to us!"

"It was just a little distraction, Ma," Isaac murmured.

"No more shooting around here. Now, let's eat this food before it gets cold."

Isaac concurred and brought the cans to the table. They slurped down the canned meats and vegetables quickly then sat in silence. All they could hear was the wind pattering against the glass windows.

"There's two rooms upstairs," Mary explained. "Little John and I took one, and you two will have the other." Mary paused, glancing at Isaac. "Don't worry there's a nice chair in your room as well."

"Thank you, Mrs. Cohen," Lucia smiled, sliding out of her chair. "I'm going to bring some things to the room."

After Lucia left, Mary concentrated on Isaac. "You know, Orsdel always thought of you as a son," she said, tearing up. "He didn't deserve anything that happened. He was trying to make that town a better place!"

"I know, Ma," Isaac replied calmly. "They'll pay. They'll all pay." Mary began crying, and Isaac gave her and Little John a warm hug. "We should all get some rest."

Isaac walked up the stairs and found his room. He opened the door to Lucia sitting on the bed adjacent to a window. After giving an awkward wave of acknowledgment, he strode over to the shabby arm-chair and tried to get comfortable in it.

Lucia looked over to him. "We have to go back. We can leave Mary and Little John here. There's food for weeks."

Isaac smiled dimly. "Not tomorrow," he began. "But I know. Anyway, I'm going to go to sleep."

Lucia hesitated then leaned back against the headboard. The window whistled from the warm breeze. "You know, this bed is probably big enough for the both of us," Lucia said.

"That's alright. I won't bother you, " Isaac responded.

"It's no trouble, really. You'll probably sleep better here."

"Are you sure? I only take your offer becaus—well... laying down would do me some good after riding all day."

"Of course."

Isaac stood up in the dark room and made his way over to the opposite side of the bed. He pulled the sheet out and slid under. They both stared stiffly at the ceiling. Lucia eventually rolled over on her side, her back to Isaac. Isaac glanced over at her and closed his eyes. After a little while, he felt a soft hand brush his arm. Lucia gently pulled his arm over her in a caress. Isaac smiled and held on to her for the rest of the night.

— — —

He woke up sprawled across the bed, his eyes forced open by the low rays of dawn pouring through the window. He watched Lucia sleep for a moment then sat out. The momentary solace in his own mind had given way to a morbid truth. Orsdel was dead; Kit was likely dead; and his home was unsafe. Isaac carefully slipped off the bed and left the room. He quietly walked through the bright hall and down the stairs, careful not to wake the others. After grabbing a can of beans, he stepped onto the porch and gazed into the open field. Shortly thereafter, he made his way to the barn to see Ruth.

The great mare rested silently in the stall Isaac had left her in. As he approached, she rose and leaned her head out. Isaac lightly stroked her mane and quickly gathered some hay to bring to her stall and the stall of Lucia's horse. As the horses started eating, Isaac opened the canned beans he had brought. They soon finished, and Isaac opened the stall doors to let the horses run free. He took a few steps outside the barn to observe the horses gallop in the morning light. Isaac watched them dance in circles then walked back toward the house.

The house was still quiet; there was no noise but the creak of Isaac's footsteps up the stairs. He slowly opened the door to the bedroom and picked up his saddle bag. Isaac paused to look down at Lucia but promptly continued out the door. Downstairs, he took his repeater and some additional rations. Without a look back, he left the house in search of Ruth. The white mare was still running in the grand pasture next to the barn.

"Here, Ruth!" Isaac shouted. "Let's go, Ruth!" The horse galloped over to him. Isaac stowed his items on her back and climbed on. After pointing her north, they set off.

PART 2

~

The true life of John Cohen was a mystery to
many. Although Orsdel had known John since the war,
there was an unspoken past that his old friend carried
with him. John was born to a large family in Maine, the
oldest of six. Because of this, he became the protector of
his younger brothers and sisters. Their mother Elizabeth
was a lovely woman who spoiled her children. On
Wednesdays, she baked sweet bread for them; at the end
of the week, she brought them to the local circus; and
after church, she played games with them in the field
behind their house. She loved her family, and she didn't
approve of the harsh hand her husband Jeremiah ruled
with.

Jeremiah was a hard man. He had a specific view
of how his children should conduct themselves, and when
this was infringed upon, he punished them. The
punishments almost always fell upon John. Jeremiah
would use an old *cross* of his to scrape into John's pale
skin. By the time John grew up, his chest was covered in
scars of his father's disciplining. This was not the only
reason John wanted to leave. He sought adventure. He
was tired of living under the requirements of a strict
society. Staying in Maine meant becoming a lawyer or

doctor, both of which John loathed. Seeing no way out, he planned to run away to the frontier. He had no ill intentions for his family until a fateful night came.

It was the day before John had planned to leave. John was outside chasing his youngest brother, William. John took pity on William for being the youngest in the family. He frequently took him fishing and even helped him with his schoolwork. John made sure William never had to experience their father's oppression.

Later that day, John and William went inside their townhouse to eat. Jeremiah had been waiting for them at the table with the rest of their family. His father was drunk. John could smell the familiar stench from the door. But this night was worse somehow. John didn't know it then, but his father had just lost a sum of money gambling and, coupled with his intoxication, was full of demonic fervor. "You're late, *John*," Jeremiah spat. "You know what happens now. Come here."

John gritted his teeth and walked toward his father. "Yes, father," he obeyed. But just as Jeremiah pulled out his sharpened cross, Elizabeth stood up.

"Not at the dinner table, Jeremiah. They're only a little late. There is no need for this!" she exclaimed.

"Sit down, Elizabeth," Jeremiah murmured, holding back his temper.

"I will not! Put that away so we can eat," Elizabeth shouted back. Jeremiah didn't take his wife's words well and sprang up in a fit of rage. He suddenly grasped the cross and struck Elizabeth across the face with it.

"I told you to not interfere, you bitch!" Jeremiah screamed. He turned back to look for John, but his son was already gone. "Where is that damn boy!" Jeremiah yelled at the rest of his children. They each sat wide-eyed in their seats, unsure what to do. But soon John had returned, holding his father's prized rifle. John slowly raised the gun, and before his father could speak, he shot him in the chest. Jeremiah staggered for a moment then slumped back in his seat. Blood gushed from his wound, and after a few meticulous blinks, he died.

"You're better off without him," John croaked to his terrified siblings. He then picked up his bag and left.

It would be months before John made it to the Illinois frontier. In the meantime, he took to stealing to keep himself alive. Sulking in the corners of markets, he could snatch a loaf of bread or two. Eventually he could hunt well enough to survive, and when he passed through Ohio, he changed his name to Cohen to erase the trail of his crime.

Back in Maine, the Plummers were broken. Elizabeth had to continue raising her younger children while accepting a job as a farmhand for money. Although they missed their father, most of the children knew what type of man Jeremiah Plummer had been. The abusive drunkard was going to Hell one way or another, and to the older children, this was just a shortcut. This was not the case, however, for young William Henry Plummer. His prayers strayed from virtue and instead sought vengeance. When William came of age, he volunteered as a deputy in their town. Unaware of John's distant location, Henry thought he might find his lost brother. Despite not having success in the endeavor, he continued his training with the law.

William killed his first man at eighteen: a common thief. The sheriff in his town admired William's commitment. Since there was another William who served as a deputy, the sheriff began calling him by his middle name: Henry. The name stuck as Henry grew into a formidable lawman. For the first time in years, Henry had a new objective. Leaving his brother's life to fate, he trekked across the country to the Montana territory. Hoping to live off gold, Henry camped out in Virginia City for many months. He continued working as a deputy while he was there, aiding the Montana Vigilantes in their search for countless outlaws.

On a stormy summer day, Henry was told to travel to a smaller town near Virginia City to meet his fellow deputy who handled the law of the area. The town was called Nevada City. Henry rode over to the town saloon, where he met with the deputy. They talked at a dusty table about a certain Red Yager who had been starting trouble just outside the town's bounds. Red had earned his name from the stories of his lethal shooting. His crimes extended all the way to California. People would say he was the best gun in all of Montana. The outlaw was rumored to be hiding at a creek's bend near Nevada City.

As the deputies finalized their plan of action, Henry noticed a lone man sitting at the bar. The morning light pinned the man's narrow silhouette against the adjacent wall. At first he didn't recognize the face, but as the man turned, he realized it was his *brother*. Unable to react, Henry glared at him. It was like seeing a ghost from his past. He could only watch as John took a final sip from his murky glass and left. In that moment, something reignited in Henry. An old malice was restored.

That evening, Henry followed the deputy to Red's reported whereabouts. They happened upon a small tent sitting under a tree. There was a fire with meat burning next to the camp. The deputy crept up upon the tent while Henry watched. There was a ruffle from inside, and Red emerged from the canvas in his nightwear. The deputy cocked his revolver and pressed it into Red's head. "We have you now, Yager!" the deputy seethed.

Yager laughed. "Took ya boys long enough," he yawned, looking over at Henry. "I surrender. Here are my hands."

The deputy pulled out his rope and tied Red's hands. "You filthy bastard," the deputy scoffed. "We ought to give your body to the pigs!"

"Sure does sound interestin," Yager replied, rubbing his hands together. "Can we go now? I'd like a ride."

"We should go," Henry said to the deputy.

"I'm not finished," the deputy growled. He lowered his revolver to the fire and stared into the flames. "Got some fine meat cooking here. Don't mind if I take it, do you?"

Yager shrugged. "Not goin to be much use to me anymore."

The deputy laughed, forking some meat off the skewer. "You shouldn't be so quick with that tongue," the deputy said, raising the glowing tip of his revolver. Henry trembled.

"Hey!" Yager shouted. "Don't do that. Don't do that!"

"Keep that mouth open, Red!" the deputy screamed.

"Stop this! AH!" Yager shrieked, the metal burning his tongue into pieces.

"Stop it," Henry said, stepping toward the other deputy. "Stop!" Henry yelled. He hastily pulled out his revolver and aimed at his partner.

"What are you doing, Henry!" the deputy began. "Put that thing down!"

"No," Henry said coolly. The deputy let out a sharp breath and turned back to Yager. He tried to raise his gun back to Yager's bleeding face, but Henry shot first. The deputy stumbled down and fell into the fire. Henry walked over to Yager and removed his binds. Yager gave a subtle nod of gratification amid his tremors. Henry sighed and gazed at the dead deputy's face burning in the charred logs. "I'm going to need your help, Yager," he said.

The night quickly gave way to a sunny morning. Yager had mostly recovered from his wounds but wasn't too keen on talking to Henry. They shared what was left of the meat, and then Yager started packing up the camp.

"Are you really an outlaw?" Henry asked bluntly. "I expected more fight in you."

"You really a lawman, *Henry*?" Yager snapped back, fastening his bed roll to his horse. "In my experience, they don't go around killin their partners."

Henry furrowed his brow. "Fair enough," Henry paused. "But seeing as I saved your tongue from that deputy, you're coming with me."

"And where is that?" Yager questioned.

"Back to Nevada City," Henry continued. "Need to deal with an old friend."

Yager groaned and picked up his remaining things. Henry walked over to the deputy's horse and pulled off its saddle. With a swift whack, he spooked the horse away. Henry then jumped onto his black stallion while Yager scrambled onto his own horse. They spun the horses around and started in the direction of Nevada City.

They first rode through a valley of dense grasses. On either side of them was a string of rolling hills that seemed to float to the horizon. Eventually, the rough grass became a trail. The horses quickly adjusted to the dirt path and quickened the pace. Several travelers passed the pair, and fortunately, they weren't recognized.

At nightfall, they arrived in Nevada City. Lamps lit the main road that consisted of a saloon, hotel, and hardware store. Across from the building was a shallow gully that had a few tents in it. Henry and Yager hitched their horses next to the saloon and stood in the alley. Behind the saloon, there were rows upon rows of small houses.

"His name is John," Henry muttered. "I don't know which home is his, so we'll check them all."

Yager sighed. "Well off you go. I'll take the north side."

Henry nodded and walked to the south; he started with a rather large house in a corner. He straightened his badge and knocked. There were soft footsteps nearing the door, and a flustered woman emerged. "Why hello, sir! What are you here for?" she asked, glancing at a wrist watch.

"Sorry to bother you, I was just wondering–"

"Who in God's name could be here at this hour, Martha!" a voice shouted from inside the house.

"I'm sorry," Henry stammered. "There doesn't happen to be a John here, does there?"

"Well, yes!" she exclaimed. "What could you want with him?"

"He's an old friend of mine, you see." Henry explained. "You wouldn't mind if I had a word with him?"

"That's all fine, but how'd you manage befriending—" she was interrupted by a young boy pulling at her hand. "Huh, here he is now!"

Henry chuckled. "A common name," he said. "Apologies for my disruption." Henry hastily jogged away from the residence and approached the next home.

Another disgruntled resident answered and told him off. After a dozen homes, Henry had no luck. He decided to regroup with Yager, but after searching the dark streets, Henry couldn't find him either. Hopeless, he strode back toward the saloon. He could hear drunk men howling into the night. Just as Henry turned the corner to where his horse stood, a voice caught his attention. The voice was coming from a cabin just behind the hotel: it sounded like John, or at least what he remembered John sounded like. Henry paused for a moment or two, then turned and made his way to the home. He let out a long exhale and knocked.

After a few minutes, a young woman pulled the door open with a boy's hand in hers. "I'm sorry, sir! My boy Isaac has been acting up all day!" the woman sighed.

"That's quite alright, Miss," Henry smiled, some sense of relief pouring over him. "I'm sure this doesn't concern you, but is there a John that lives here?"

"My husband John you mean?" she replied.

Henry coughed sharply. "Right, your husband. Where might I find him?" Henry asked.

"You just missed him! He left for Fort Benton yesterday. He'll be there for a month working on a new map of the territory."

"Thank you, Miss," Henry said, lowering his eyes to the ground in guilt.

"Of course," she said, closing the door with a grin.

Henry came away from the door in a nervous stroll. He turned into the alley and immediately heard Yager's feral laugh in the saloon. Unamused, Henry strode inside and didn't stop until he was at Yager's crowded table. With an unwavering glare, he dispersed the group that had been playing cards.

"I see the search went well for you," Henry finally remarked.

Yager grinned. "You'd be a lot more fun with a bottle of whiskey, ya know that?"

"No time for that. We set out tomorrow morning for Fort Benton."

"Benton's a long way from here," Yager commented. "What makes ya so sure he's there?"

"Found his kin in a cabin. They said he just left, so we ought to catch him on the trail."

"Well, seems you've got this figured out. I'll be ready in the mornin," Yager said, slumping back with his glass.

"I'll get us rooms next door," Henry announced as he stood up.

Yager groaned in compliance, and they left the bustling saloon. After a short stroll, the men arrived at the hotel. It was a musty old building made of pine like the rest. Henry stepped off the creaky walkway to the entrance and pushed the door open.

"Hello?" the young man at the counter asked.

"Hey," Henry said dully. "Two rooms,"

"Sure," he said, examining a document. "That'll be a dollar for the night."

"Fine," Henry muttered while he searched his pockets.

"You two aren't from around here, are you?" the man asked with a nervous smile.

"I think just those rooms," Yager said, grinning sarcastically.

"Yes, sir. Here you are,"

Henry and Yager took the keys and made their way to the rooms. "Dawn," Yager declared, and after exchanging nods of agreement, they retired.

The morning was brisk. The sun was just peeking over a distance ridge when they awoke. Henry was the first one up. He hammered against Yager's wall then began collecting his belongings. Making his way to the dresser, he put on his flat-brimmed hat and picked up his revolver. Its black steel had degraded since he'd last studied it in Virginia City. He pulled out gun oil from his bag and started rubbing it on the barrel. Despite his tedious efforts, the barrel maintained its tarnish.

"Let's ride, Henry!" Yager shouted from outside the door. Henry stood up and holstered his gun. He then picked up his bag and marched out the door.

"We'll follow the Missouri River north. That's probably the trail John took," Henry explained, stepping outside.

"Who is this John anyway?" Yager asked. "Seems yer going through a hell of a lot of trouble findin him."

"He's my brother. Or he once was. He lost the right to family the day he killed our father."

Yager snickered. "I'll find him. Ya better be ready when I do."

Henry nodded, and they unhitched their horses. With a kick, the pair set off east toward the river. At the end of the town, they picked up their speed. Henry rode alongside the gulch that had established Nevada City in the first place. Many people knew the story of the few lucky miners who had struck it rich at this very gulch. The town prospered as thousands migrated in search of gold. The same story described Virginia City, which Henry and Yager were coming up on. Virginia City was significantly larger than Nevada City in both size and population.

The two men rode in through the main street. There were a few folks wandering the streets who recognized the young deputy's return.

"How'd it go, Henry?" an old man asked from the walkway.

"Alright," Henry answered anxiously. He was eager to leave the area without attracting any unwanted attention.

"I heard the sheriff was expecting you! You ought to go down to the office," the man exclaimed. The man then shifted his focus to Yager. He turned his head quizzically at the outlaw's presence with Henry. "Son, who's your partner here?" the man questioned Henry.

"Just a traveler," Henry said quickly. Before the man could respond to the obvious lie, another mounted man approached.

"Sheriff," Henry nodded.

"There you are, Plummer! Say, did you see where that deputy from Nevada City went? He was supposed to be here yesterday," the sheriff said. "Hey and who is this you got here?"

Yager slowly lifted his shrouded face into view. "Hello, Arthur," he smirked.

"Goddammit, Henry! You were supposed to hang this man!" the sheriff yelled in anger.

"No, sir, wai–" Henry tried to continue, but it was too late. Yager had already raised his rusty revolver and pulled the trigger. The bullet struck the sheriff in the chest.

"Hah!" Yager shouted. "Take that you cockeyed bastard!"

"Why'd you have to do that!" Henry barked at Yager. "Now we have to get out of here! Let's go!"

Yager chuckled as they raced toward the town's edge. "Ol Arthur killed my old partner. Figured I could return the favor!" Yager said, letting out a low growl.

Henry shook his head. "We're after a different man! We don't need law following us all the way to Fort Benton!"

Behind them came a trampling of hooves, and three men emerged, guns in hand. Henry forced his horse to a faster pace as the pursuers caught up. The man in front held up a long rifle. Henry whipped his arm back and fired a few armless bullets. One of the shots managed to strike one of the riders, but Henry's horse also gained a flesh wound in the exchange.

Yager noticed a thick patch of forest on the left side of the trail. "Cut left, Henry!" he shrieked with a devilish grin. They rode off the path and were soon in the trees. The lawmen behind them lost their way, giving Yager and Henry a chance to regroup. "Get down," Yager commanded Henry. "We're gonna surprise them," he muttered. Yager then tied his own horse behind a wider tree and pulled off his repeater.

Henry did the same with his injured horse and glanced behind them. "I see one," Henry noted. "There's the second, they're both coming this way."

"Duck below that log there," Yager said. "We'll jump out when they're near." Henry tucked his head below the rotten log and gripped his revolver. Yager cocked his repeater and glimpsed around the side of his tree cover. He nodded to Henry as the sound of clapping hooves returned.

Just as the lawmen were entering the trap, one of them noticed Henry's hitched horse. "Hold up," the man murmured to his partner. The men slowed their horses into a walk. They examined the surrounding trees but couldn't make out the fugitives. The leading lawman led his horse toward Henry's fallen log.

As the horse stepped over the trunk, Henry lifted up his revolver and unleashed his full cylinder into the horse's abdomen. The man screamed in pain as several bullets penetrated his body. Yager lunged out from his tree and finished the injured lawman. His partner frantically tried to shoot at Henry, but his shots collided with the log. Henry placed his empty revolver on his chest and crawled closer to his cover.

"Run off, boy!" Yager advised the last lawman. "Live another day! Hell, live two!"

The lawman glowered at the tree from which Yager's voice came. "You... you killed him!"

"And I'll kill you too! So get!" Yager shouted. Henry, still prone behind the log, reached for the fallen lawman's corpse.

"Come out you demon!" the lawman yelled, raising his revolver to Yager's tree.

"If you insist!" Yager growled, cocking his repeater. He sprung out from behind the tree and was surprised by a gunshot to his left. The last lawman fell back on his horse, dead. Henry stood up and tossed the rifle he'd stolen to the ground.

"Come on," Henry said, grabbing his horse. "The river's this way."

Yager raised his eyebrows. "Ya sure ya weren't born an outlaw, son?"

"I'm no outlaw. But a badge won't have me discriminating against the condemned," Henry muttered.

"Whatever you say, *Plummer*," Yager smirked. Henry glanced at his Yager but said nothing.

The river appeared on the horizon as they left the forest. Broken sunlight beamed down on the water in an angelic ray. Henry listened to the river's rising chorus. Once they made it to the bank, Yager dismounted to drink some of the cool water.

"Upstream, there was a settlement I passed a while ago. We'll stay there on the way to Fort Benton," Yager explained. "Should be a couple days ride."

Henry nodded and gazed at their lengthy path. It was a subtle, worn trail next to the river's edge that seemed to extend forever. Yager promptly stood up and mounted his horse. The pair then set off northward.

There were many stormy days and bitter nights by the time they made it to the settlement. The locals called it "Last Chance Gulch" after its prosperous gold claims. The south edge of the town was cluttered with men, horses, and wagons when Yager and Henry rode in.

"A place this big ought to have a hotel. Can hardly feel my back after being on this damn horse so long!" Yager gripped.

"I'll get the stallion's wound looked at while you sort our rooms," Henry replied as Yager made his way deeper into town. He then turned around and looked at the buildings behind him. There was a large stable to the right, where the wagons were congregated. Henry dismounted and led his black horse over.

"Hey, Mister," Henry said to the man inside. "Can you take a look at my horse?"

The man looked up from the dirty horse shoes he was cleaning. After a moment of analysis, he turned his head toward the back of the stable. "Ned! We got another shot horse out here for you!" he called.

A younger stableman hastily appeared in the doorway. "What do you need now, Eli!" Ned pried. The man had long light brown hair and wore an old hat.

"Name's Henry. It's my horse that needs helping," Henry told the man.

Ned sighed. "Well in that case, bring the beast back here," he said, gesturing to an open stall.

Henry nodded and led the horse in. "He's been shot," he explained. "Doesn't seem to have done much to him though."

Ned laughed. "What kind of business were you getting into, partner?"

"Just some outlaws," Henry said, flashing his badge. "Anyway, I'd hate to put down the animal–"

"Where you headed?" Ned interrupted eagerly.

"Doesn't concern you," Henry answered. "Do you have ointment for the wound?"

"Right. Yes I do." Ned walked away and ruffled through a nearby shelf. He pulled out a jar of dark paste. "This ought to help it," he claimed. "And hey, if you ever need a hand on the road, you know where to find me." Ned placed the ointment in Henry's hand and left the stall.

Henry watched Ned leave while he opened the jar. After applying the ointment to the horse's wounded hind, he walked into the street. A brisk wind swept heaps of dust into the air. Henry strode past several mounted men onto the walkway.

"Well who's this fine lawman?" one of the men snickered.

"You're in the wrong camp, *Deputy*," another seethed.

Henry flashed a grin at the men and continued toward the hotel. It was a dainty building with a low roof and a broken door. Yager's hoarse voice could be heard a fair distance away. Henry stepped inside and noticed the young woman he was chattering with.

"The rooms?" Henry asked Yager.

"Oh and here's my partner, Mr. Plummer," Yager exclaimed to the woman. "He's a bit of a serious one, I wouldn't look him in the eye!"

Henry forced a laugh and picked up one of the keys Yager was holding. "Don't go drinking all night. We leave early."

"Yes, Sir!" Yager mocked with a smile.

Henry found his room around the corner from the lobby. He sat on the bed and exhaled. It wouldn't be long before they'd catch John. Henry hadn't seen his oldest brother in years. He didn't know how John had lived with himself all this time. Abandoning his family and murdering their father all in the same day. The thought made Henry clench his fists and slowly flex his fingers straight. The only sure thing was that John's days were numbered.

118

– – –

A screaming voice outside roused Henry from his respite. The room was dark and filled with moonlit shadows. Henry heard Yager fire insults at the other voices. Making his way to the window, he examined the argument taking place. Yager, whiskey in hand, was stumbling in the street with a firm finger raised.

"You cheatin bastard!" the taller man yelled.

"Can't lose with the cards you two gave me!" Yager refuted loudly. Silence ensued as the men contemplated their next actions. Henry reached for his revolver and placed it on the window sill. Before he could react, the taller man swiftly drew his revolver and loosed a shot into Yager's side. Henry and an injured Yager both raised their weapons but a third shot first.

Ned the stableman walked into Henry's view from the walkway. The remaining man attempted to wake the tall man, but he was gone. Ned kept his gun trained on him and made his way to Yager. "You hurt bad?" he asked.

"What the hell!" Henry yelled after sprinting outside.

"Just fine, partner," Yager replied to Ned, clearly ignoring Henry.

"Get inside, you ought to bandage that wound," Henry commanded. Yager huffed and shuffled to the hotel door. "And you," Henry said, turning to Ned. "Quick shooting."

"The finest gun in the gulch," he smirked. "You know, seein as your partner is hurt, I could come with y—"

"We don't need you," Henry claimed. "You'd better clean up this body before the wrong person sees you."

Ned nodded wistfully and began to pull the dead man's legs. He didn't make it far with the body before Henry returned.

"You know the way to Benton?" he asked.

"Of course," Ned said eagerly. "We buy horses from a trader up there."

"Alright, you can help us get there. But once we make it, the deal's done."

Ned nodded. "You won't regret it, Sir."

"Henry."

"Henry," Ned smiled.

Before long, the three men were on the trail. Yager wore a tight bandage on his crusty laceration while maintaining a steady groan. "Some men just don't know when to quit gamblin," he grumbled, examining his side.

"Maybe if you lost every once in a while, they'd stop," Henry pointed out.

"Aint my fault they didn't see the fifth ace. They should of been payin attention."

Henry sighed, and they rode on for some time without talking. All that could be heard were the spring birds chirping at each other and the river humming quietly to their right. The sun's heat that beamed down on them was sent away by a northern wind.

"Quite a horse you have there," Henry eventually commented to Ned.

"Figured I'd borrow it from Eli for a while," Ned sneered. "He doesn't seem fit to ride anything but a donkey."

"You're not going back after Benton?"

"I think I'll go to Mexico. They say they have the prettiest women down there!" Ned grinned.

"Well don't pass through that camp with the man's horse on your way south."

"Aint likely," Ned laughed. "What are you doing in Benton anyway?"

"Bounty," Henry muttered.

"Didn't take you as the law type. Must be some man."

"Is that so," Henry seethed back in a brewing annoyance.

Ned went quiet, looking down at the muddy path ahead. "I once knew a lawman by the name of Wyatt Eisley. He'd track fugitives in California. He was stern in his work, never let any of them get away. When I met him, he didn't seem like a lawman. Farmer, maybe. But then his own son killed the neighbor's daughter. They say it was an accident, no one really knew. Anyhow, next day I saw Eisley march his boy up to the rope. The whole town watched him hang. I guess, even though he didn't look it, he was the real law type. Letting justice tear his family apart and all."

Henry glanced at him. "And where is Wyatt Eisley now?"

"Can't say for sure. He left to go north right before I went to Utah."

"What a story, *boy*!" Yager interjected sarcastically. "Sounds like a real scary man! But just so you understand, you're coming with us to shoot men like him, not admire em!" Yager wheezed, gripping his side.

Ned drew his revolver smoothly and looked at the sky. Two crows were passing above them. He quickly aimed the iron barrel of his revolver up. He pulled the trigger once and slammed his other hand on the hammer, firing an additional bullet. Both birds gracelessly fell from the sky. "That's what I'd do to Eisley," he jeered.

"Don't believe I'll live to see the day," Yager groaned.

"Slow," Henry commanded, his eyes searching the ground. "Those look like fresh tracks."

Ned bowed his head to find what Henry was talking about. "One horse and it ought to be close," Ned affirmed. "Could it be who you're looking for?"

"Can't be sure. Could be Indians, they're the only other people on a trail this far north."

The men rode forth, noticing more and more the tracks left by a single traveler. The pasture across the river was suddenly occupied by a great herd of bison. Some of them roamed to the river's edge and drank the clear water. Henry stared at the beasts as they grazed. They seemed quiet; even the river's slow drag drowned out their low tones. Shortly thereafter, they passed the herd. Once more, Henry shifted his focus to the muddy path before them.

Abruptly, a piercing scream interrupted the silence of the trail. It came from behind them. From the bison. Henry pulled his horse around to examine the cause of the commotion. There were five bare-chested men galloping at the bison. Two of them carried bows while the rest had spears.

"Blackfeet," Yager spat. "Those Indians think they own the territory!" Yager pulled out his revolver while staying in a cramped posture.

"That won't be necessary," Henry said. "They're hunting the herd, not us,"

The spearmen stood up on their horses as they neared the bison. One man jumped off, impaling his target through its neck with a stone blade. The bowmen corralled the herd and sent arrows hurling toward the animals on the outside. The last Blackfoot to gallop through the pasture did not attack the bison, but instead, rode toward Henry, Ned, and Yager. Across the water, he slowly nodded at the three men. Henry returned the acknowledgement and slapped down Yager's poised weapon.

The men departed from the scene and a warm rain began. The horses trudged through the muddying earth with a fair bit of grunting. Henry watched a flock of distant crows soar toward them. They flew together in a rigid line, but eventually, one bird on the outside dove down. It appeared like a dark spec in the bright sky. The bird glided toward them elegantly and finally chose a thick branch ahead of them to perch. Henry stared into the crow's glassy eyes. When it was out of sight, he settled into his saddle and continued forth uneasily.

– – –

The blue sky was replaced by a crimson gloom and then darkness. The silent ride on the path was interrupted by a figure ahead of them. It was a solitary rider, his face half concealed by a white scarf.

"Easy," Henry whispered to his companions. "Let me see who is up ahead."

"Do you think it's–" Ned hissed back.

"Quiet, I'll handle it," Henry replied, dismounting his horse. He hastily hiked toward the traveler through the muck. Before announcing his presence, Henry recognized the cross pin on the man's scarf, the color of his unkempt hair, and even the posture with which he rode his horse.

The man turned his head, clearly hearing Henry's heavy footsteps. "I heard a story that you were in Nevada City," the man said, revealing a smile. "I wish I'd found you sooner, *brother*."

"How can you sit there?" Henry spat. "You know why I'm here. Not even the devil himself could forget what you've done."

John grew serious. "Our father was a waste of life. Perhaps your loyalty to him blinded you to that truth."

Henry stared at his brother in a growing fury. He placed his right hand on the grip of his revolver. Ned and Yager approached the brothers and stood silently.

"Don't think you're winning any battles here," John said calmly. He lifted up his arms, exposing an empty belt. "You were better off without him, Henry. But this is all in the past! We can finally be brothers once more. Join me in Fort Benton. I'm meeting a friend there, and he surely has room for you and your boys."

"No," Henry grunted, tears looming in his eyes. "You couldn't be my brother after you killed Father, and you can't now!" Henry instantly drew his revolver and aimed at John.

"Hey!" John yelled vehemently. "There's no need for that!"

"Do it, Plummer," Yager murmured from behind them.

"You're better than that," John said to Henry. "You're better than *me*."

"How would you know!" Henry cried. "I've killed men before!"

"I know. It's in our blood. But you have the power to choose."

"There's no choice. I have to do this!"

"I'm sorry, Henry. I should've just left. But the man you see before you isn't the same one who killed Father. I've changed."

Henry lowered his arm. He wiped his tears away and slowed his frantic breathing. "So have I," Henry whispered. He snapped up his revolver and shot John in the chest.

His brother let out a croak and lowered his frightened eyes to the wound. "You're no brother of mine," he breathed.

Henry screamed and unleashed the rest of his bullets on his brother, who fell off his horse onto the ground. Henry ran back to Yager and snatched his revolver. He paced toward John's corpse and shot him six more times.

"He's done!" Ned shouted, but Henry continued, loading his own gun once more to further defile his dead kin.

"Boy's lost his damn mind," Yager sighed. "We'd better get outa here soon."

"I know a place we can go," Ned said. "It's a gold camp a few days from here. I rode through it when I came to Last Chance Gulch. No law there either."

"I guess that means yer comin," Yager said. He looked down at Henry, who was now toying with his brother's cross pin. "Ya finished, son?"

"He had it coming," Henry muttered. "He had it coming."

"I'm sure he did, but we've gotta leave now. We can't have the wrong person seein us here."

"He's right, Henry," Ned affirmed. "Let's get riding."

PART 3

~

The sky had grown dark. Bannack would appear on the horizon at any moment, but Isaac's mind was elsewhere. No matter how long he stared at the path in front of him, he couldn't help but think of Lucia. Her kind smile appeared in his eyes. He wondered what she'd done that morning. Did she miss him?

Moriah came into view first, followed by the wooden structures of Bannack's southern edge. The mountain hovered over the town like a warden of the west.

Just outside of town, Isaac observed a figure riding out toward him. He gripped his revolver as the man met him.

"Is that you, Isaac?" a familiar voice asked.

"Wyatt?" Isaac replied. "What are you doing out here?"

"You can't go back, Isaac. Not now. Most of the townsfolk were spooked by that shoot out. The town's overrun with outlaws. The law won't do anything because... well, they're outlaws too."

"I have to go back. If what you're saying is true, I need to get my friend out of there. Then I will end Plummer."

"Listen to me, Isaac. Come with me: I'm going to Idaho to rally some lawmen to ride with me back to town. Your friend will be fine."

"I can't leave him."

"You stand no chance. There are more members of the Innocents than you know. Now that Plummer's given his act up, they would all come to his side in an attack."

"How do you know about the Innocents?"

Wyatt looked down. "I was once a lawman myself, but that was before. Isaac, now is no time for bravery."

"Plummer killed my father, Wyatt. And Kit is the best friend I've got. I *have* to do this."

"You don't," Wyatt sighed, pulling out his two revolvers. "But if you're going to, I'm coming with you."

Isaac smiled bleakly then grew earnest. "I have a plan."

– – –

Isaac and Wyatt hitched their horses to a nearby tree and crept toward town. They sulked through the shadows, dodging the street lanterns' dim glow. Eventually, they arrived at the back of Skinner's Saloon. Isaac gave Wyatt a nod, and the older man passed him and made his way to the proximal apothecary. As Wyatt looked for Kit, Isaac slowly snaked through the alley and snatched one of the street lanterns. Carefully, he laid the lantern in a bed of tinder next to the saloon's foundation and picked up a rock. While Isaac was setting up his distraction, a drunk had roamed into the alley.

"What you doin there, boy?!" the man shrieked.

"Quiet!" Isaac whispered desperately, but the man came closer.

"I will not!" the man announced, turning to the street. "Hey boys–"

Isaac smashed the rock onto the man's head before he could finish his call. The man fell to the earth and blood began pouring through the wound. Isaac watched the man die for a moment then quickly hit the lantern with the bloodied rock, igniting a small blaze.

Wyatt looked through the apothecary window and saw the saloon catch on fire. A dozen men ran out, and a crowd gathered to watch the spectacle.

"Who are you?" Dr. Leavitt interrupted from the shadows.

"Hey, Mister, you wouldn't happen to have a Kit here would you?"

"Who is he to you?" Leavitt asked.

"Noone," Wyatt ascertained. "I'm helping get him out of town before the Innocents decide they want him."

"A friend of Isaac's, I presume?"

"I suppose so, yes."

Dr. Leavitt smiled. "He's upstairs. You'll need to help him walk, his sickness hasn't quit."

"Right," Wyatt said. "Thank you."

Upstairs, Wyatt found Kit groaning in his room. He gripped Kit's shoulder, rousing him from his dazed state. "We're going to Isaac," he said firmly. Kit could only nod in agreement, his strength gone. Wyatt pulled Kit's limp arm over his own neck and managed to shuffle out of the room. Kit's feet clapped the stairs as they descended.

"Good luck," Leavitt smiled at the pair. "You'll want to take the back door."

Wyatt thanked the doctor and exited with Kit at his side. The sick boy shook vigorously in the cool air. Down the line of buildings, Wyatt noticed Isaac ducking in the shadows. He lugged Kit forward, stopping before each alley to make sure there were no onlookers. Isaac gave Kit a gentle embrace when they met next to the burning saloon. "Look who's still alive!" Isaac grinned. "We've got to get you out of here. Let's head for the stable, it should be empty at this hour."

Kit gestured in agreement, and Wyatt began to pull the boy toward the distant stable. Isaac lagged behind the pair and glanced at the crowded street. Riding on his black stallion toward the chaos was Henry

Plummer, his black cross glimmering in the firelight. Ned Ray flanked him with a revolver drawn.

"What's going on here?!" Plummer bellowed above the horde. Immediately, several men approached the sheriff to tell him embellished stories of what couldn't have happened.

Isaac discreetly slid out of the alley and caught up to Wyatt and Kit. "Just a little farther," he whispered to Kit, who was already slowing down. Isaac took Kit's other arm, and with Wyatt's help, they dragged him to the stable. Inside, Kit's old horse was sleeping. Wyatt quickly shook it awake and began saddling it. Just as the horse was being prepared, a man from the street saw the three men in the stable.

"Hey, boys! You wouldn't happen to be the ones the sheriff was looking for would ya?" he grinned evilly.

"We aren't, Mister," Isaac claimed. "Leave us."

"Oh I will, *boy*, but I'm bringing the sheriff back with me!"

Isaac tried to follow the man before Wyatt stopped him. "We get your friend out first. You'd be a fool to face that crowd alone."

Isaac let out a sharp breath of frustration then went back to setting the horse. Soon, they were ready to get Kit going. After a couple of attempts, they managed to sling him over the saddle.

"Ride out to the homestead, Kit. You have to make it there, you know the way," Isaac said adamantly. He then slapped the horse's hind, making the animal rush down the path out of town.

"They're coming," Wyatt reported and unholstered his dual revolvers.

"Get out of here," Isaac said, readying his repeater. "It's not your fight."

"I've been running from this for too long, son," Wyatt muttered. "It's *always* been my fight."

They walked out of the stable as the crowd approached, headed by Henry and Ned. "Thought you'd never come back, Cohen!" Henry laughed. "Do us a favor and get out of town, will you?"

"Tell them why I'm here, sheriff," Isaac commanded, advancing forth with his repeater.

"The men here don't care, Isaac. They've all done worse. Hell, I've done worse!"

"Only this time your victim will be avenged!" Isaac declared.

Just then, a mounted figure darted across the street, firing a repeater toward the lawmen. It was Lucia. She danced around the returning fire and rode into the stable for cover. Ned and Henry dove behind the adjacent buildings, Ned having taken a shot to the leg from Lucia's surprise attack. Wyatt and Isaac picked off a few armed gang members within the mob then came back to the stable.

"Did you really think you could run off without me?" Lucia smiled at Isaac, sitting next to him. He smiled back, gently pulling her to him. Finally, Isaac could bear his urge no longer, and he kissed her. They held onto each other in a warm hug until they could hear more men approaching.

"We need to stay together out there," Isaac whispered to both of them. He counted down on his fingers from five, and at the fist, they bolted up and met the incoming gang members.

Wyatt took out two of them men with perfect accuracy while Isaac and Lucia backed him up with their repeaters.

"On your left!" Isaac screamed to Wyatt, who turned just in time to face his new opponent.

"Eisley!" Ned cackled, limping out into the open. "I've waited a long time for this!"

Wyatt grinend back and quickly fired at the deputy. They exchanged several bullets before Wyatt's attention was drawn to the larger battle going on behind him with Lucia and Isaac. "We've got to go back!" Wyatt yelled. "To the sta–" His voice was cut off by a dishonorable bullet to the back. His legs buckled, and he collapsed to the muddy ground.

"The famous Wyatt Eisley isn't so hard to kill after all!" Ned snickered.

Isaac instantly sprinted toward the laughing deputy. He felt every muscle in his body engage for the just execution he was about to commit. Ned fired at the incoming boy, but his shots were too slow. Isaac swung the barrel of his repeater into Ned's face, breaking several bones with a bloody *crunch*. He then thrusted the repeater down on the deputy's neck and kept it pressured. Ned's grisly face grew even more red as he struggled to breathe. He tried to kick Isaac, but it was no use. In no time, the deputy was dead.

Isaac paused for a minute then quickly returned to Lucia, who was handling the gang well. The men who were not laying dead in the street were hiding behind adjacent buildings, struggling to target their assailants in the lightless stable. On the right line of buildings, Isaac saw Henry, and now Buck, glimpsing at the action. He tried firing a bullet toward them, but it collided with their cover.

"We have to draw them out," Lucia said, turning to Isaac. "It's the only way."

"We can't go out that way," Isaac muttered with a gesture to the open door next to them.

"Out the back. We can flank them," Lucia replied.

Isaac looked into her hazel eyes. He took her hand and said, "Be careful." He pulled her to her feet and they snuck through the backdoor.

Isaac took the left flank next to the creek. Placing his finger in the bullet chamber, he ensured that his first shot would fire. The metal bullet was cool to the touch. He passed the back of the first building, then second, and then third. In the alley of the fourth building, he heard whispers.

"When are they going to come out, Buck?" one voice asked.

"How would I know, Willy?" Buck grumbled. "Just watch for any movement."

"It's all black over there! We can hardly see a thing!"

Amidst the debate, Isaac leaned around the building and fired a few shots at the unsuspecting gang members. Buck recoiled, narrowly dodging a bullet meant for him, but some of the others were less fortunate. Isaac retreated to gain cover behind the prior alley while the men tried to chase him. Again, he peeked out and let loose a barrage of repeater fire. There was a loud click with his last trigger pull. He desperately tried to reload the weapon, and as he did, he heard the shouts of men across the road.

Lucia had stumbled upon Plummer and several of his companions talking behind one of the buildings. She ran out in the street and fired at the flustered men following her.

Isaac glanced into the street as Lucia appeared from the opposite alley. He finished loading and returned to where Buck had been covering. There was a writhing man among the dead in the alley but no Buck. Isaac swiftly raised his repeater and killed him. He then walked through the alley into the street where Buck, Henry, and several others were taking shots at Lucia.

Lucia twirled around the gunfire and was able to take out two men on Henry's side of the street. Soon, Isaac was on her side of the road again. They walked with their backs together toward the stable, shooting anything in view.

Isaac saw Buck's hat behind a corner just a few feet behind them. "I'm going for Buck," he shouted back to Lucia. Isaac walked away and surprised Buck in the alley while he was trying to reload a revolver. "What are you doing?" Isaac asked. But before Isaac could finish his taunt, Buck drew a second revolver from his back and shot Isaac in the side. The bullet felt like a coal had been thrust inside his body. He stumbled away from the alley and clutched his wound. Buck followed Isaac away from the alley despite being far behind. When Buck turned the corner to the creek bank, he was met by the barrel of Isaac's loaded repeater. With a blast of smoke the deputy's head was degraded to a stump.

Isaac flexed his abdomen to ease the pain, which seemed to work in the short term. He tied his overshirt around the wound and ran back to the street. Lucia was fending off the gang with ease. She shuffled between her cover and fired back with vitality. Isaac joined her in the battle once more. He could no longer see Henry, though he kept a watchful eye. Lucia proceeded to where the men were hiding, and she and Isaac shot the last few from point blank range. Isaac let out a sigh of relief. All he could do was grin at Lucia. He turned away from her to examine the dead bodies in the mud.

There was one final gunshot. Isaac swung back around. Lucia gasped. She clutched her chest, blood already staining her dress.

"Lucia," Isaac mouthed. He caught her as she fell to the ground. She gripped his hand and convulsed violently. He stroked her soft cheek. "Stay here, with me!" he begged, tears streaming down his dusty face. Suddenly, her tremors stopped, and she was dead.

Isaac looked up, still holding her limp body. Henry stood next to the stable with his blackened revolver raised. "Any last words, Cohen," he called through the moonlight. Isaac froze. He gently let Lucia's body down to the ground while maintaining eye contact with Henry. The same moment Isaac ducked, the sheriff fired. Isaac swiftly sprang to his feet and kicked his grounded repeater up to his hands. He returned Henry's fire, hitting him in the leg. The sheriff shouted in pain and limped hastily toward the crumbling saloon.

Isaac used the last of his grit to chase Plummer through the street. He saw him mount his black stallion and gallop into the distance. Isaac tried to raise his repeater, but he had no stamina left. He dropped to his knees and watched his final bounty riding to Moriah.

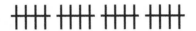

By the end of the hour, the rising sun roused Isaac from his trance. He looked down at his bloody wound. Pain flooded his body as he tried to get up. Glancing around, he was reminded of what had just happened. The dead surrounded him. He saw where Wyatt and Ned had met their fates, where Buck had been executed, and where Lucia had been slaughtered.

Down the street and into the adjacent plain, Isaac caught a glimpse of Ruth. The mare was standing in the exact spot he'd left her the prior evening. At first he walked slowly toward the mare, but after regaining some fortitude, he broke into a jog.

The mare seemed pleased to see him, although Isaac was too focused on his wound for a greeting. He tugged the makeshift bandage tightly and bit down on his shirt, grimacing in agony. He then lifted himself onto the horse slowly and headed off toward the distant mountain.

The hateful face of Henry Plummer stained his mind. Every thought was revenge. He looked to Moriah for assistance, but all he could see were black specs on its slope. One of the specs was moving. Isaac could barely notice its changing position. It appeared to be crossing the face of the mountain. He locked his eyes on the target and hastened Ruth into a gallop.

— — —

Before reaching the base of the mountain, Isaac encountered a tall thicket of pine trees. He carefully navigated Ruth through the woods, trying to catch a view of the spec through the canopy. Soon, they emerged in a boulderfield. Isaac could now make out the minute features of a man on a horse. Renewed with faith, he kicked Ruth forward. The mare slipped on the rocky path, almost jerking Isaac off the side. He was forced to dismount and lead Ruth up a smoother route.

After a short distance, the mountain flattened out. The ground was now covered in a thick moss that Ruth could ride on. Isaac tilted his head up and saw Henry above him, nearly in shooting range. "PLUMMER!" he screamed. The man looked down at him for a moment then continued across the face.

Isaac forced Ruth into a tired trot. Below him, he viewed the miniature town of Bannack as well as the hills that enveloped it. While distracted, a gunshot echoed off the mountain's face. Isaac spun his head up. Henry had made it to the ridge and was now taking shots at him from cover.

Isaac jumped off Ruth and slapped her into a retreat. He planted his feet firmly in the rugged turf and raised his grimy repeater. The radiating cross on Plummer's chest served as a mark for Henry's bullets. He loosed several bullets as suppressing fire and took more steps toward Plummer's direction. From this distance, Isaac's repeater was far more accurate than Henry's revolver. The sound of several more gunshots rebounded off the mountain until, finally, Isaac's last shot sliced through Henry's shoulder. The sheriff cried out in pain and dropped the revolver from his limp hand.

"Enough!" Isaac shouted while reloading. "Raise your hands!"

Henry raised his left hand, unable to move his right arm. He was panting rapidly as Isaac approached the ridge. "Alrigh–" Plummer breathed. "Oka–"

Isaac glared at the broken man. He raised his repeater and pushed it into Plummer's forehead. Plummer didn't react. Isaac watched blood stream out of Plummer's shoulder and saw the dark red patch on his leg from their prior confrontation. Isaac pressed the barrel harder into Plummer's forehead and screamed at him, still without a response. Isaac's eyes welled with tears. Plummer died.

Isaac threw his weapon to the ground and took a seat. He glanced over at his fallen foe and angrily grabbed

the cross and badge from his chest. He felt the weight of
the metals in his two hands. The badge was heavier but
the cross was larger. Isaac closed his eyes. He thought
about who had carried these before him. After more
deliberation, he quickly threw both of the pins over the
other side of the ridge. He sighed and composed himself.
Next, he picked up Plummer's black steel revolver, which
he put at the back of his belt.

Isaac stood up, feeling the irritation in his side
coming back. He took one step forward and one look back
at Plummer's body slumped against Moriah's ridge.
Trekking forward, he made his way down to Ruth. The
mare seemed to know the way back to Bannack, despite
Isaac's silence.

— — —

Back in town, Dr. Leavitt was organizing a mass
burial in the hillside cemetery. Townsfolk uninvolved in
the gang activity helped carry the bodies of Plummer's
followers. Isaac approached him, asking where Lucia's
body had been placed. The doctor solemnly directed him
to the church.

Isaac walked down the street and opened the
familiar doors to Orsdel's church. Lucia's pale body was
situated just below the altar. Someone had put an

147

assortment of wildflowers around her. Isaac sat on the step in front of her and caressed her hand. "I'm—" he croaked. "I'm so sorry." He examined her tattered dress. A bloody flower had formed where she'd been shot in the heart. Isaac sat there for a while until Dr. Leavitt appeared in the doorway.

"To live in the hearts we leave behind is not to die," Dr. Leavitt said. "Thomas Campbell."

"They're all dead," Isaac whispered, entranced by sadness. "I'm merely the one that was left behind. This isn't living."

"You're right. It is not. It is mourning. But the thing about mourning is that it's temporary. It will take weeks, perhaps months, but soon, you will forget this sadness and remember Lucia in the way she was, not is."

"What happens to Bannack?"

"We remember and rebuild. There are many good people in this town, Isaac. Despite your... losses, you have helped rid this town of the vermin that corrupted it. Bannack can return to the promised land we all came here for."

Isaac scoffed. "Corruption always finds a way in. And we can't just replace everything," he glanced back at Lucia's body. "Some things can't be restored."

"That's why we need someone to protect us," Leavitt declared. "And who better—"

"No, I've had enough bloodshed for one life. I'm taking my family far away from here."

Dr. Leavitt chuckled. "I might do the same if I were you but just something to think about ."

Isaac sighed and stood up gingerly. He walked past Leavitt without a word. Outside, the sun shined down on him. No clouds could be spotted, even at the distant horizon. Isaac watched fathers, mothers, brothers, and sisters dragging the dead into a wide ditch. He rolled up his frayed sleeves and joined them.